UR-DRAMA
THE ORIGINS OF THEATRE

The publication of this work has been aided by a grant
from the Andrew W. Mellon Foundation

UR-DRAMA
THE ORIGINS OF THEATRE

E. T. Kirby

New York ● NEW YORK UNIVERSITY PRESS ● 1975

Copyright © 1975 by New York University

Library of Congress Catalog Card Number 74-32656
ISBN: 0-8147-4559-8

Manufactured in the United States of America

ACKNOWLEDGMENTS

A sketch for the chapter on the origins of theatre in India was de-livered as a paper at the conference on The Oriental Theatre of the 10th *Rassegna Internazionale Dei Teatri Stabili*, chaired by Professor Fer-ruccio Marotti, Florence, April 1974. Other parts of this work have previously appeared in print in: "The Origin of the Mummers' Play," *Journal of American Folklore*, 84 (July-Sept. 1971), 275–288; "The Origin of Nō Drama," Educational Theatre Journal, 25:3 (October 1973), 269–284; "The Shamanistic Origins of Popular Entertainments," *The Drama Review*, 18:1 (March 1974), 5–15. This material has been adjusted to the present context, slightly abridged, with omission of the informational footnotes. I have here chosen the form "noh," a common noun, feeling that use of the macron is inconvenient and an incomplete transliteration.

I would like to thank Mel Gordon and John Towsen for their help in research on magic, and Marilyn H. Strong, Associate Librarian, and Norma Lawrence of the Interlibrary Loan office, Drake Memorial Library, State University College at Brockport, N.Y., and also the Audio Visual Services section of the Educational Communications Center of the college for photographic duplication.

I would very particularly like to express my deep appreciation to the administrators of the State University College at Brockport for the released time which has made this work possible, especially to Dr. Louis Hetler and to Dr. Joseph W. Talarowski who, as Chairmen of the Theatre Department, were instrumental in allowing me to work in part for a "university without walls."

PN
2131
.K5
c.2

B

CONTENTS

v

William D. Mc'ntyre Library
University of Wisconsin - Eau Claire

436593

INTRODUCTION: GENERAL THEORIES OF ORIGINS

Considerations of the origins of theatre often still remain trapped in a myth created at the end of the nineteenth century, a myth in the Frazerian sense of an institutionalized, commonly accepted fiction based on "mistaken explanations of phenomena." The twelve volumes of Sir James Frazer's *The Golden Bough*, which first began to appear in 1890, presented a vast spectacle of primitive vegetation magic identified with certain archetypal events understood to have characterized the primal, worldwide ur-religion of mankind; a sacred marriage, a scapegoat, a divine king slain and resurrected to produce fertility. Equating Zeus and Hera with the folk customs of Europe that played so large a part in his vegetation analogies, Frazer observed them to be "the Greek equivalents of the Lord and Lady of the May" (Frazer, 131). The great pantheon of deities that had presided over the birth of the rational mind in ancient Greece was visualized as having been created as personified forces of nature by a childlike, poetic fancy bemused by seasonal change.

> Year by year in his own beautiful land [the ancient Greek] beheld, with natural regret, the bright pomp of summer fading into the gloom and stagnation of winter, and year by year he hailed with natural delight the outburst of fresh life in spring. Accustomed to personify the forces of nature, to tinge her cold abstractions with

the warm hues of imagination, to clothe her naked realities with the gorgeous drapery of mythic fancy, he fashioned for himself a train of gods and goddesses, of spirits and elves, out of the annual fluctuations of their fortunes with alternate emotions of cheerfulness and dejection, of gladness and sorrow, which found their natural expression in alternate rites of rejoicing and lamentation, of revelry and mourning. (Frazer, 416–17)

It is difficult to avoid the impression that Frazer wanted his readers to participate in this naiveté, while at the same time feeling distinctly superior to the capacity of the conceptual mind as it was exercised in the ancient world. It is reasonable to doubt, as a general theory, the primary instrumentality of seasonal change in the lives and metaphysical practices of so-called primitive peoples. Yet seasonal ritual, in which "the community did everything in its power to facilitate and insure spring's return," has often been assumed to have been acted out in a series of ceremonies, protodramas which then evolved into theatre directly, by structuring its form, and/or indirectly, by giving its pattern to myths. Benjamin Hunningher described this genesis of theatre from communal vegetation magic in *The Origin of the Theater* (1955) as follows:

Through often repeated communal and mimetic dance-ritual, the tribes did everything they could to attract new life which they longed to receive. As soon as the spring appeared in nature the entire community hurried to welcome it and strengthen its power by an elaborate representation of its victory over winter and summer. The battle between winter and summer is of primary importance in the development of primitive religion as well as of the theatre. Frazer's numerous examples demonstrate how, through annual repetition of these rites, the idea of a definite seasonal change retires to the background and winter-in-general gradually opposes summer-in-general, death opposes life. . . . From this concept arose the performance of the year-king or year-priest, known over the whole world, who overcomes death to bring life. With the approach of winter the year-king himself turns into the daemon of death and must perish in a duel with the champion or king of the next year for life to spring forth anew. (Hunningher, 17–18)

Gilbert Murray and Francis Macdonald Cornford had used material of this type as the foundations of their theories of the origins of tragedy and of comedy in ancient Greece; both tragedy and comedy had been based upon an agon, or combat between the seasons, and upon the death of a year-king or year-god. The combat in the mummers' plays has been taken as evidence of a sacred battle between the seasons, and we will have reason to question this concept in more detail later. Frazer's five examples of European folk customs representing a "battle of summer and winter" are on the order of the game played by two boys, which is "a scuffle between the two little boys, in which Summer gets the best of it, and turns Winter out of the house" (Frazer, 324). The single other example, an Eskimo tug-of-war, is incorrectly reported from the sources used. Franz Boas, the ethnologist, changed his view in the 1901 report and observed that the winter people (the Frazerian negative principle) should win (Boas [E], 141). Far more significantly, there has never been any evidence that kings or their representatives were killed yearly to perpetuate fertility, and the incidents at Nemi, which were supposed to show this, pertained to gladiatorial combat rather than to the hypothetical year-cycle king. (Fontenrose, 8ff.). The alleged African examples seem to be fabrications, much like the amusing information about the talking lion that kills the king, clearly given by informants who wanted to please the researcher who explained such "totemism" to them (Tremearne, 32ff.).

> So constantly is it said that the killing of kings "used to be," and so unverifiable is the rare report of contemporary king-killing, that one may conclude that the whole reported tradition of African king-killing is itself mythical, a fragment or memory of an ancient African myth.
> (Fontenrose, 11)

The year-king or year-priest, "known over the whole world," was derived from interpretation which sought to find everywhere the reflection and multiplication of a certain image. As John Peale Bishop put it:

> ... however wide we wander, however deep we delve into the records of the past [contained in *The Golden Bough*], we are always coming up against one being, the Vegetable God, who as the decapitated Texcatlipoca or the dismembered Osiris is strange, but who is not strange at all, once our astonished gaze has recognized the likeness, as Jesus.

Christianity is seldom mentioned; there is no need it should be,

for Sir James naturally assumes that the main articles of the
Christian faith are known to his readers.   (Hyman, 253)

Anthropology has found the image of the year-cycle vegetation god
to be a synthetic one, assembled from data abstracted from its meaning
within the context of the culture. Ruth Benedict, for example, questioned Frazer's methodology.

> Studies of culture like *The Golden Bough* and the usual compara-
> tive ethnological volumes are analytical discussions of traits and
> ignore all the aspects of cultural integration. Mating or death prac-
> tices are illustrated by bits of behavior selected indiscriminately
> from the most different cultures, and the discussion builds up a
> kind of Frankenstein's monster with a right eye from Fiji, a left
> from Europe, one leg from Tierra del Fuego, and one from Tahiti,
> and all the fingers and toes from still different regions. Such a figure
> corresponds to no reality in the past or present.   (Menagh, 236)

The purpose of assembling information in this way was to show that
the ur-religion of primitive peoples had been a proto-Christianity based
on the "ritual pattern" of vegetation magic centering on the Christlike
image of a slain and resurrected spirit of fertility.

> Thus, in very truth, along this line of reasoning, Christ came not to
> destroy, but to fulfil; to give a new and higher significance to those
> age-long rites and beliefs by which the world was being prepared for
> the final revelation "when the fulness of the time was come." On
> this hypothesis, it might be argued that God left not Himself with-
> out witness throughout the ages, the Holy Spirit working through
> the ancient pagan systems in order to prepare the world for "greater
> things than these." Regarded from this standpoint, Christ becomes
> the Heir of the ages, and the ritual pattern the divine scheme for the
> redemption and reconciliation of the human race to God.
>   (James, 325)

There is beauty in the magnitude of this concept, but we know that
faith should not force its support from data meant to be considered
rationally and without bias. Two events in the "ritual pattern" which
Cornford proposed had been the basis of comedy were a sacrifice of the

combatant in the year-ritual and the eating of a feast which was curiously like Holy Communion in the Roman Church.

> . . . a Sacrifice and its usual sequel, the cooking and eating of a Feast, are incidents [that] . . . fill in the outline of the action between the Agon at the beginning and the Marriage at the end. . . . We have seen sufficient traces of an older form of ritual in which it is the God himself, in human or animal form, who is the victim. He is dismembered, and the pieces of his body are either devoured raw in a savage omophagy, or cooked and eaten in a sacramental feast.
>
> (Cornford, 98, 52–53)

This was based upon the standard Frazerian concept of primitive totemism, in which it was supposed that the animal, identified with vegetation fertility, had been sacrificed and eaten to absorb its potency. Jane Ellen Harrison attributed to Robertson Smith the insight that eating the totem animal had prefigured Christian sacraments: "In a splendid blaze of imagination his mind flashed down the ages from the Arabian communal camel to the sacrifice of the Roman mass" (Harrison [T], 136). In his study of totemism, the noted anthropologist Lévi-Strauss has cogently expressed his reservations in regard to this concept and its context:

> In order to place the modes of thought of the normal, white adult man on a firm foundation and simultaneously to maintain them in their integrity, nothing could therefore be more convenient than for him to separate from himself those customs and beliefs, actually extremely heterogeneous and difficult to isolate, around which had crystallized an inert mass of ideas which would have been less inoffensive if it had been necessary to recognize their presence and their action in all cultures, including our own. Totemism is firstly the projection outside our own universe, as though by a kind of exorcism, of mental attitudes incompatible with the exigency of a discontinuity between man and nature which Christian thought has held to be essential. It was thus thought possible to validate this belief by making the inverse exigency an attribute of this "second nature," which civilized man, in the vain hope of escaping from himself as well as from nature itself, concocts from the "primitive" or "archaic" stages of his own development.

... In amalgamating sacrifice and totemism, a means was found
of explaining the former as a survival or as a vestige of the latter,
and thus of sterilizing the underlying beliefs and ridding of any
impurity the idea of a living and active sacrifice, or at least by
dissociating this idea to distinguish two types of sacrifice, different
in origin and meaning.   (Lévi-Strauss, 3)

The hypothetical "ritual patterns" that were said to have produced
theatrical form were essentially analogues to the rise and fall of dramatic action, conflict, and resolution. Any number of different rituals,
not associated with vegetation magic, could provide evidence of a
similar generalized pattern. But it is in this sense, applied to the literary
aspects of drama rather than to the origins of theatre as enactment, that
ritual theory is now most often encountered. Northrop Frye and Susan
Langer describe literary genres as if they were somehow structured by
the "rhythms" of seasonal progression. Theodor Gaster, in recognizing
some of the excesses of ritual theory applied to specific works, has
turned to this more generalized concept.

It may, for instance, be quite wrong to assume that a particular
Hittite or Canaanite or Scandinavian myth, play, or epic actually
goes back, in point of literary genealogy, to an earlier ritual libretto;
but it may nevertheless be quite right to assume that this particular
type of composition was inspired or conditioned in the first place
by the standard pattern determined originally by those of the primitive performances. In other words, what is really at stake is not the
dependence of a particular composition upon an actual performance, but rather the parallelism between a pattern of narrative and
a pattern of ritual, or—to put it in broad terms—the ultimate relation of a genre of literature to a genre of ceremony.   (Frazer, 464)

We have no evidence of these "earlier ritual librettos," but all of
literature is thought to be their heritage. The "genre of ceremony" is
vegetation magic, but there is little viable evidence concerning what
these rituals might have been like in the ancient world, or how they
structured literature, other than through the doubtful Fazerian concept
of personification of natural forces. The theory that the origins of
theatre can be identified with year-cycle rituals remains a modern
"myth."
Detailed and generally convincing refutations of theories of the

origins of drama put forth by followers of Frazer absorbed much of William Ridgeway's attention and energy. In contrast with the Frazerian method, which reorganized data abstracted from their cultural context, Ridgeway concentrated on locating various forms of drama within their cultural contexts, paying particular attention to those aspects determined by non-Western religious beliefs. His *Dramas and Dramatic Dances of Non-European Races* (1915) was the first work of its kind in the English language, and it has remained the only work to concentrate at all upon the origins of non-Western theatre. The drawback to Ridgeway's method, which is still perhaps a necessary evil, is that too much consideration must be devoted to the cultural context in which the particular dramatic form occurs. His work was also founded upon a particular thesis, establishing the hypothesis that theatre had originated in worship of the dead. Ridgeway proposed that Greek tragedy had originated in hero cults based on worship of the dead, a concept which could seem to be borne out by the protagonists who are represented and by the pervasive use of lamentation as a specific mode. Consideration of the *ta'ziya* passion play, which commemorates an Islamic martyr, provides one very clear example of Ridgeway's theory of origins, although the drama appears in general somewhat similar to the *Ramlila*, which honors Rama, a mythological hero. Ridgeway's concept could seem to be supported, in a sense, by examples and information which have been developed since his time, such as the number of cultures in which the affective spirits (or gods) are identified as ancestors, or the use of ancestor masks for performances and for social control in Africa. But there are other variables which would also have to be considered. Mortuary ceremonies, like other "rites of passage," such as coming-of-age ceremonies, are frequently dramatic (Charles [R], but there is very little to suggest that dramatic activity on these occasions was formative of any more advanced modes of drama.

Of particular significance to us, however, is the attention Ridgeway paid to the performances of trance mediums, with examples cited from Burma, China, Japan, and Africa. He thus arrived at a second general theory, the "doctrine that the actor was originally a medium," and it is this concept that will here be developed in detail. However, the relationship between the performances of trance mediums and the theory that theatre originated in forms that honored the dead is incommensurable. Ridgeway's primary example was the *nat-kadaws* (nat-wives) of Burma, who are possessed by "spirit-husbands" who are, in fact, legendary or symbolic dead, given identity as spirits by the nature of their deaths. But this identity does not entirely define the characteristics or nature of the performances, and it does not apply to shamanism and trance mediumship, as such.

Another general theory was outlined in Loomis Havemeyer's *Drama of Savage Peoples* (1916), which surveyed a range of hunting ceremonies, rainmaking ceremonies, initiation ceremonies, dramatic war ceremonies, and the pleasure plays of primitive peoples, but without describing any of these in detail. Examples of enactments or imitations of actions served to illustrate "an axiom upon which all the history of the drama is based . . . the fact that the desire to imitate is a universal human trait, although it does not appear to the same degree among all races of men" (Havemeyer, 241). This desire to imitate is said to be an instinct, with examples found in the behavior of animals, such as cats and dogs, and in the play of children. Gesture is visualized as having preceded spoken language, apparently as direct expression of the instinct to imitate, and it then became a necessary supplement to verbal communication. Sympathetic magic, such as acting out the killing of the animal before the hunt, is said to be based on the instinct to imitate. As a general theory, Havemeyer's stress upon imitation as a primary function in acting and dramatization is so usual as to appear axiomatic, but its actual validity is limited.

In regard to the concept that gesture preceded speech, "one can only wonder that so much recognition is accorded today to so purely speculative a theory (Spencer, Allport, Stout; Paul, van Ginneken and others)" (Révész, 51).

> In all probability human language incorporated within itself from its very inception all the characteristic constituents of fully developed speech—that is, on the one hand, the sounded word with meaningful content, together with its phonetic and rhythmic formal properties (articulation, intonation, rhythm and melody) and, on the other hand, the natural eloquence of the human body, gestures, motions of the hand and arm, facial expression and pantomime.
>
> (Révész, 59–60)

This passage reminds us how close normal life has always been to dramatic activity. But when theatre first separated itself from ordinary life, did it do so in order to imitate existent reality? In the dramatic animal dances of the Mundurucú of South America, as reported by

Robert F. Murphy, "the men give very realistic imitations, first of the peccary then of the tapir, and finally of other game animals" (Zerries, 266). H. von Becker describes an animal dance of the Leagua of South America in which the dancers "execute a number of figures which are unmistakably stylized imitations of the movements of game animals" (Zerries, 275–76). The problem is represented by the contrast between "realistic imitations" and "stylized imitations." It would seem that the origins of theatre can be directly identified with stylization, "imitative" or not, and with the abstract rather than with the realistic. Neither of the dances cited seems to have used masks or elaborate costumes, and it is these which appear to be characteristic of primitive dramatization of persons all over the world. The animal masks of the Cubeo and Cáua of South America have human faces because they represent the spirits of the animals and are hooded knee-length garments with sleeves made of bark and painted with geometrical designs (Zerries, 301). The jaguar dancer of the Bororo of South America wears a mantle painted inside with geometrical designs, an elaborate headdress made of feathers, and a mask made of woman's hair (Zerries, 271). Clearly, the intention is not to "imitate" animals. The intention is toward abstraction in style and the representation of abstractions as concepts. One of the reasons for such masks and costumes can be seen in the noninstrumental nature of the "conventionalized display" which Roy A. Rappaport has observed to be a characteristic of ritual which has analogues on an animal level.

Ethologists have also used the term ritual to refer to animal displays, some of which bear close formal resemblance to human rituals. Animal rituals are likely to involve stereo-typed, apparently non-instrumental postures and movements, and, as apparently useless paraphernalia are often manipulated in human rituals, so apparently useless biological structures are often waved, vibrated, suffused with color, or expanded in animal rituals. Like human rituals, animal rituals seem to occur under specified circumstances or at fixed times, and some animal rituals, like some human rituals, occur only in special places. . . . For a signal to be effective it must be distinguishable from ordinary instrumental activity. The more bizarre the ritual movement of structures the more easily may they be recognized as ritual.   (Rappaport, 63)

This principle would run counter to imitation, since for the "signal" of dramatic action to be effective "it must be distinguishable from ordinary instrumental activity." This point will be considered further later.

It would appear, however, that the origins of theater constitute an area of investigation that has been somewhat neglected. Perhaps comparison and generalization need no longer be deterred, as some feel they have, by "the generally unproductive labors" of Frazerian theory and method, whose work "represents for many a monumental exercise in futility" (Lewis, 12). Fine practical and conceptual field work has continued to supply vital new information which illuminates the subject directly or provides the means by which the origin and early development of forms can be reconstructed with some degree of accuracy. While certain information has been irretrievably lost, and some aspects of reconstruction must depend, as they have in the past, upon circumstantial evidence, the network of this evidence will continue to draw tighter. It is with this understanding that I will sketch first the outlines of shamanistic theater and its influences and then show the development from shamanistic rituals of a number of theatre forms in different areas of the world.

LIST OF ILLUSTRATIONS
AND SOURCES

UR-DRAMA
THE ORIGINS OF THEATRE

Chapter I

SHAMANISTIC THEATRE:
Origins and Evolution

The shaman is a "master of spirits" who performs in trance, primarily
for the purpose of curing the sick by ritualistic means. Hunting magic,
vegetation magic, conveying souls to the realm of the dead, divination,
and the giving of oracles are among the specialized functions that the
shaman assumes. The distribution of shamanism among primitive
peoples is virtually worldwide, and it has continued to exist side by side
with developed religion or as a function of it. Despite Mircea Eliade's
suggestion that we are not to think of shamanism as "primordial," there
are several reasons to consider it so. The apparent diffusion of
shamanist practices from Central Asia and Siberia through the Americas
to the very extremity of the southern continent would attest to the
great age of the phenomenon. Siberian-American shamanism represents
the metaphysical practices of hunting peoples, strongly suggesting that
the "mastery of animal spirits" was practiced by the nomadic hunting
cultures that preceded cultivation. Andreas Lommel has traced prehistoric shamanism from the Early Magdalenian (13000–6000 B.C.) by
means of the art and artifacts of the early hunters. Weston La Barre and
others have made similar identifications in regard to mankind's earliest
art. It also seems probable that shamanism occurs at times through
parallel development rather than diffusion, because of the great and
similar need and the similar structure of the psyche.

Shamanism seems to stand in a particular relationship to spirit

1

mediumship. Eliade defines shamanism as a technique of ecstasy characterized by trance flight to spirit worlds and by a mastery over fire in rituals (Eliade, 4ff.). In this state the shaman does not become the instrument of the spirits but maintains control over them. Spirit mediumship, dominant in Africa, is possession in trance by a spirit who speaks from within the medium and determines his actions, essentially an "inhabitation" or "incarnation" of the spirit. I. M. Lewis, however, has questioned the distinction, feeling that Eliade was "seeking to drive a wedge between spirit possession and shamanism" (Lewis, 50), and Rahmann has hesitated in regard to its applicability. The two modes of practice can exist in the same culture, as they do in China, and Jan de Groot reproduces an historical Chinese document which appears to discuss a cultural transition from trance flight to spirit mediumship (de Groot, 1191). Definition can include the two modes; "The term 'shaman,' borrowed from the ethnography of Siberia, means a magician, healer and spirit medium combined, a person who is able to put himself into trance states in which he is thought to travel in heaven or in the underworld or to be possessed by spirits from these places" (Zerries, 311). For our purposes, shamanism and spirit mediumship are identical, for they result in similar performances, affect audiences in the same way, and produce similar theatrical elaborations. On the other hand, it is shamanism as it is most rigorously defined which has almost invariably been the antecedent of established theatre forms. It is on this basis then that we may speak of the shamanistic origins of theatre.

That shamanic performance may be considered the ur-theatre or prototheatre implies a very important distinction. Shamanistic ritual is unlike rites-of-passage or other forms of what may be called ceremonial ritual in that it depends upon the immediate and direct manifestation to the audience of supernatural presence, rather than its symbolization. All ritual and ceremony can be theatrical, but the theatricality of shamanistic ritual is related to its function in a particular way. In order to effect a cure of the patient, belief in what is happening must be held, reinforced, and intensified, not only in the patient, but in the audience as well, for their experience contributes directly to the effect. The audience actively reinforces the experience of the patient, and its own belief in a particular world view or cosmology is in turn reinforced by direct experience of it. Shamanistic theatre, founded upon manifestation of supernatural presence, develops from a small curing seance, which in effect needs only patient and shaman as participants, but actually depends upon an audience. This leads to more elaborate curing ceremonies and to rituals and trance dances for curing, exorcism, and other purposes. This complex develops finally into performances which are purely theatre, spectacles from which the functional element has disappeared. We may first trace a number of the significant aspects of performance and reconstruct general evolutionary sequences in this development, beginning with the basic element, the curing seance.

Lucile Hoerr Charles's study of 1953, "Drama in Shaman Exorcism," drew attention to the theatrical aspects of the shamanistic seance. Examples in her cross-cultural survey were drawn from Asia, Africa, North America, South America, and Oceania, and the summary of her findings reads as follows:

> Professional cure by a shaman who is the central actor usually involves careful preparations, full publicity, and an eager audience; impressive setting and lighting, costume and makeup, theatrical properties and sound effects. Actual performance includes dramatic invocation of evil or benevolent spirits, or both, for diagnosis and advice as to treatment; possession of or battle with the shaman by the spirits through ecstasy or frenzy which may be considered a supreme example of dramatic impersonation, often with elaborate use of voice, dialogue, and body pantomime; concretizing the disease demons, and driving them away, often with sucking out, sleight of hand, and display of disease objects; and luring home of the sick person's soul. The performance may require the help of stage assistants, and active participation by the patient and the audience. . . . The audience experiences entertainment, enlightenment, comforting, and renewed faith; and, occasionally, reactions of skepticism. The shaman afterwards may be exhausted, and collapse is common. Theatrical measures and paraphernalia throughout heighten the emotional quality of the seance and powerfully assist the shaman's psychotherapeutic function. (Charles, 96)

The shamanic performance can occur indoors or out, in various types of setting or staging, during the night or during the day, but a rather small, darkened room, dimly illuminated, seems to be characteristic of the prototypical seance. The walls that contain the seance have the spirit world behind them; it can howl about outside, rap upon them, cause them to shake, and penetrate into the darkened, enclosed space. Close proximity to others gives the audience some reassurance. Close proximity to the shaman who will manifest the supernatural brings a

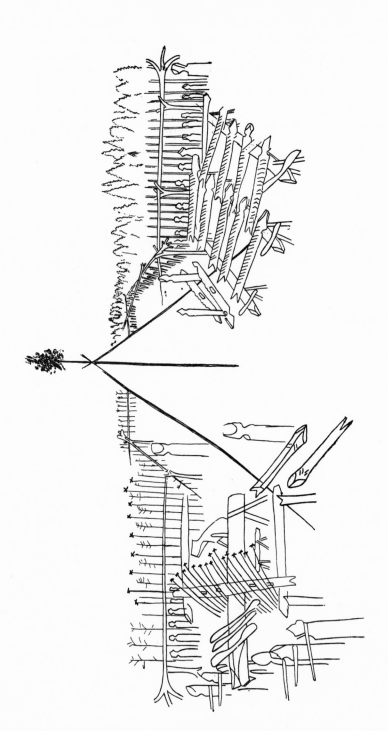

1. Sketch of the arrangement of furnishing of an Evenk shaman's tent showing tree center pole and wooden guardians of the "road" to the spirit world.

degree of terror. The Evenk seance is typical of Siberian shamanism.

At this moment, the song ceased and the sounds of the drum were gradually muffled, becoming a soft roll. The listeners with bated breath awaited the appearance of the spirit. The ensuing silence was broken by a sharp blow on the drum, changing into a short roll. In the silence following this, the voices of the spirits could be clearly heard: the snorting of beasts, bird-calls, the whirring of wings, or others, according to the spirit appearing before the shaman at the moment. . . . The journey of the *khargi* [an animal spirit helper] to the other world is described in the shaman's songs in such fantastic form, so deftly accompanied by motions, imitations of spirit-voices, comic and dramatic dialogues, wild screams, snorts, noises, and the like, that it startled and amazed even this far-from-superstitious onlooker. The tempo of the song became faster and faster, the shaman's voice more and more excited, the drum sounded ever more thunderously. The moment came when the song reached its highest intensity and feeling of anxiety. The drum moaned, dying out in peals and rolls in the swift, nervous hands of the shaman. One or two deafening beats were heard and the shaman leaped from his place. Swaying from side to side, bending in a half-circle to the ground and smoothly straightening up again, the shaman let loose such a torrent of sounds that it seemed everything hummed, beginning with the poles of the tent, and ending with the buttons on the clothing. Screaming the last parting words to the spirits, the shaman went further and further into a state of ecstasy, and finally, throwing the drum into the hands of his assistant, seized with his hands the thong connected to the tent pole and began the shamanistic dance—a pantomime illustrating how the *khargi*, accompanied by the group of spirits, rushed on his dangerous journey fulfilling the shaman's commands. . . . Under the hypnotic influence of the shamanistic ecstasy, those present often fell into a state of mystical hallucination, feeling themselves active participants in the shaman's performance.   (Anisimov [S], 101–2)

Dialogue, enactments, ventriloquism, incantations, music, dance, and song create a swirling stream of images drawn from a number of performance modes. The effect is literally hypnotic and hallucinatory, as we see also from Shirokogoroff's account of a Siberian Tungus seance.

The rhythmic music and singing, and later the dancing of the shaman, gradually involve every participant more and more in a collective action. When the audience begins to repeat the refrains together with the assistants, only those who are defective fail to join the chorus. The tempo of the action increases, the shaman with a spirit is no more an ordinary man or relative, but is a "placing" (i.e. incarnation) of the spirit; the spirit acts together with the audience, and this is felt by everyone. The state of many participants is now near to that of the shaman himself, and only a strong belief that when the shaman is there the spirit may only enter him, restrains the participants from being possessed in mass by the spirit. This is a very important condition of shamanizing that does not however reduce mass susceptibility to the suggestion, hallucinations, and unconscious acts produced in a state of mass ecstasy. When the shaman feels that the audience is with him and follows him he becomes still more active and this effect is transmitted to his audience. After shamanizing, the audience recollects various moments of the performance, their great pychophysiological emotion and the hallucinations of sight and hearing that they have experienced. They then have a deep satisfaction—much greater than that from emotions produced by theatrical and musical performances, literature and general artistic phenomena of the European complex, because in shamanizing, the audience at the same time acts and participates.   (Lewis, 53)

Seances in other geographic areas can differ considerably from those of Siberia, often being less overtly spellbinding, but they develop the situation and the narrative of the cure in relation to the spirits and have definite aesthetic and theatrical qualities. John Beattie and John Middleton comment in regard to the spirit mediumship of Africa on "the degree to which spirit mediumship is, or may be, no more—and no less—than a kind of drama, differing perhaps in the degree of involvement (or dissociation) of the actors, but essentially a theatrical performance" (Beattie and Middleton, xxviii). Dialogue, the hallmark of our drama, occurs in the seance as the shaman converses with his spirits or recounts the adventures of his trance journey to the spirit worlds. It also takes place in the form of interaction between the spirits and the participants in the ritual. This dialogue can be achieved by the ventriloquism of the shaman, as among the Tanala of Madagascar, described by R. Linton.

The people begin clapping and singing softly. After a time a knock-
ing is heard on the walls, or voices are heard repeating: "We have
come. We have come." There are sometimes as many as ten or
twelve spirits, distinguishable by their different voices. The voices
are nasal and seem to come from the east or west . . . sometimes
high, sometimes low. . . . The head of the family, or the sick person,
then tells the spirits why they have been called. After this the
ombiasy [shaman] explains the situation fully and the spirits tell
the cause of the illness and the medicine to be given. . . . After
answering the questions, the spirits drink the rum, dance and sing
. . . accompanied by rhythmic rappings on the floor and walls, but
always near the ombiasy. . . . Finally they say they are tired and
must go, and troop off noisily. The spirits are the souls of ancestors,
but no individuals can be identified.   (Charles, 109)

Dialogue also occurs when a spirit possesses or inhabits a shaman, as
among the Yakuts, where the shaman in this example converses in
trance with the master of the house in which the seance is being held.
The spirit comes seeking a gift as propitiation.

The shaman rapidly approaches the entrance, beats the drum
three times and repeats "Ba-ba-ba-ba," shaking his head.
"My one-sided Keeleeni, my one-eyed lame one, come quickly."
He goes to the audience, holding the drum behind his back and
begins to speak in the name of his control, the spirit Keeleeni,
stuttering:
Shaman (spirit): For what need have you caused me to be called.
Master of the House: I was not able to withstand the morning frost
and evening dew.
Shaman (spirit): How will it be if you give me a present. If you will
give me something I will have yours who ran away and will bring
back yours, who went away!
Master of the House: Next time when you come!
Shaman (spirit): Is it because of that (I) am scampering away with
nothing, eh?
The shaman goes to the left, mutters something (lets the spirit out
of him) and speaks, without stuttering, in his own name.
                                                        (Popov, 266)

A series of spirits then inhabit the shaman in turn, each carrying on a dialogue with the master of the house and seeking a gift as propitiation for leaving the patient. This pattern of dialogue, in form and content, is remarkably similar to that found in the Ceylonese *sanniyakuma* demon play, an exorcism which leads directly to drama, as we shall see. It would also appear that conversation with the spirit developed into the shamanic functions of giving oracles as prognostication, divination, or advice. There is a transcript of an interesting dialogue between two trance mediums in Bali which served to provide oracular advice to the community (Belo [B], 119). Dialogue must be considered a vital and active aspect of shamanist dramatic performance.

Another primary factor in the aesthetics of these performances is a magical illusionism capable of inducing not only belief in the supernatural, in the virtually impossible, but of contributing to a state of mind which further augments the actual spectacle with hallucinatory perceptions, as in Siberia. The shamanistic seance is aptly named. It is very like the seance of a medium in present Western culture, with its levitation on tables, strange rappings, spectral apparitions, and voices from the dead. Eliade notes how in a Chukchee shaman's seance "suddenly the voices of the 'spirits' are heard from every direction; they seem to rise out of the ground or to come from very far away. . . . During this time, in the darkness of the tent, all sorts of strange phenomena occur: levitation of objects, the tent shaking, rain of stones and bits of wood, and so on" (Eliade, 255). In an Evenk seance in Siberia "wild screams, the snorting of beasts, bird voices rushed about the tent with the shaman" (Anisimov [S], 104). Shamans of the Algonquins used ventriloquism to represent rushing wind and the voices of spirits underground and in the air (Hoffman, 138–39). Hallowell describes the characteristics of an Ojibwa seance as follows:

When a conjurer undertakes to divine, a small structure is built and, upon entering it, he summons his spiritual helpers. They manifest themselves vocally, the voices issuing from the conjuring lodge being distinguishable from the voice of the conjurer who kneels within. Each *pawagan* [spirit] upon entering the tent usually sings a song and sometimes he names himself. . . . Another manifestation of their presence is the movement of the lodge itself. From the time the conjuror enters it is seldom still. It oscillates and sways from side to side, behaving in a most animate fashion.

(Hallowell:10)

South American shamans of the Mundurucú carry on similar dialogues with the animal "mothers" while alone in a hut (Zerries: 265). In South Africa, ventriloquism is associated with a pseudo-shamanism, itinerant performances developed from the functional rituals (Gelfand: 106). It seems likely that shamanism represents the actual, as well as the metaphorical or archetypal, origin of ventriloquism as a form of modern Western popular entertainment. The same is true of the various forms of "magic act," the visual illusionism which accompanies this auditory illusionism.

As the phenomenon of the shaking tent and the appellation "conjuror" in Hallowell's description suggest, the shaman employs techniques similar to those of the stage magician. One sleight-of-hand trick in particular is characteristic of shamanism the world over, the apparent extraction of the disease agent from the patient in the form of some material object—a bone, stone, or tuft of fibers—that has been concealed in the shaman's mouth or about his person and is produced at the crucial moment. That this simple trick is a characteristic of rituals in differing cultures is undoubtedly due to a need to make the disease both tangibly and conceptually real within a system of causality that can be dealt with by the shaman. Related tricks used by Algonquin shamans include carved representations of snakes produced from a cloth bag that has been shown to be empty, and one in which a bear's claw is made to hang "magically" suspended from the inverted surface of a mirror (Hoffman, 97,99). Alaskan shamans use a whole range of sleight-of-hand tricks in their practices of curing.

One observer describes "driving a knife into the body without marking the skin; bending a long, narrow piece of nephrite; swallowing a bead and later on recovering it from another's ear or eye, and tricks with twine cut into lengths, chewing the pieces, amid heaving of the chest and violent contortions, and drawing the twine out entire" (Lantis, 88).

Among his tricks, the Alaskan shaman swallows eighteen inches of a smooth stick, an act suggesting the origins of sword swallowing (Lantis, 88). In the pseudo-shamanism of the Shango festival in Nigeria, sleight-of-hand is employed to extract yards of cloth from beneath the shirt of an unsuspecting audience member (D. W. M., 309). Such conjuring, an apparition of objects, is directly associated in shamanism with the techniques of the escape artist. The Cree shaman allows himself to be stripped nearly naked and tied tightly within an elk's skin. After a lengthy incantation, he escapes suddenly from his bonds (Hoffman, 142). Ojibwa shamans "will permit themselves to be securely tied, placed within the jugglery, and a moment later be at liberty and the cords at some other locality" (Hoffman, 143). The practice is also common throughout Alaska, where it is elaborated upon in terms of spectacle and real-life drama.

Getting untied when he had been trussed in various ways and allowing himself to be burnt were favorite shamanistic tricks around Norton Sound and south of the Lower Yukon. In one such case, the shaman, bound and wearing a large mask, was placed inside a crib of wood, which is set afire. However, his assistants secretly substituted a log of wood for the shaman. At Cape Prince of Wales, instead of being strangled, a shaman might be burnt, put down through a hole in the ice (where he supposedly remained for several months), or speared or knifed without injury.   (Lantis: 88)

A Kwakiutl shamaness appears to have her head cut off or to be run through with a sword. She is then sealed in a wooden box which is consumed in a fire until only bones remain, and the "spirit" of the woman then speaks from the fire. The trick is accomplished with a tunnel and kelp speaking tubes that extend beneath the fire. The woman later appears unharmed, of course (Boas [S], 239; Hawthorn, 55). Many other tricks of shamanic death and return from death were played out in this way.

An informant once saw a tohwit [shamaness] of a visiting tribe begin to dance and utter cries the moment the canoe grounded, indicating her desire to have her head struck with a stone hammer. So a hammer was produced, and the woman stood in the canoe. A man raised the stone and seemed to strike her on the forehead with all his strength, and there was heard a resounding thud caused by a simultaneous blow on a heavy timber. The woman fell overboard backward and lay face downward in the water, and she remained in that situation more than an hour. The informant afterward asked the chief of that tribe how it was done, and received the explanation that pieces of bladder-kelp had been joined into a long tube, one end of which was held in the woman's mouth while the other was concealed among the beach stones.

Other ingenious feats of the tohwit involve apparent decapitation, transfixing with a spear, splitting of the shoulder with a paddle, and driving a wedge into the temple.   (Curtis, 210)

Another trick involved coloring sealskin to match the body. This was then cut and entrails hidden within it drawn out, apparently from the abdomen. The shamans of Formosa and of Tibet act out a similar invulnerability when they pretend to stab themselves, cutting open a bladder of blood placed beneath their clothes (Rahmann, 741). The "disappearance" of the Eskimo shaman is an enactment of his "leaving" in trance to visit the spirit worlds (D. Ray, 7). Magical death and revival derives from shamanic initiation in which the candidate is killed by the spirits and then given new life. Illusionism like that of the stage magician was originally proof of the shaman's supernatural control over death, a corollary of his control over disease.

The Indian basket trick, which originated in shamanist fakirism and became famous on the European variety stage, shows the direct connection between shamanism and modern illusionism. A child is placed in an oblong basket that is tied with a belt and then pierced with a sword, which emerges dripping with blood. When the basket is opened, it is found to be empty, the escape of the person inside having been effected by means of a contrivance, a sliding double-bottom and back to the basket. Sponges hidden inside produce the blood (A. Hopkins, 46–47; Jennings, 430). Southern Nigerian conjuring managed to present the illusion that a baby was pounded to death in a mortar, or that a man was impaled without effect, or that a man's head was cut off and then replaced (Clark, 120). A historical account suggests that Chinese shamans of the T'ang dynasty (A. D. 618–907) performed the type of illusionism in which a woman is sawed in half.

Yeh, a Taoist doctor of the Ling-khung convent, was wont to recite spells over his sabre, and thereupon strike therewith with all his might at the navel of his patient, across whose belly he had placed a branch of peach or willow. This branch was thus cut right asunder without any infliction of wounds on the flesh. He once struck with his double-edged sword at a woman so truly that she fell in two pieces, blood flowed all around over the floor, and the family shrieked loudly; but he placed the two halves against each other,

spurted water from his mouth on them, and uttered a spell; and in a
moment she was quite restored to her former condition.

(de Groot, 992)

There are many strange stories of this type from China, in which what
must be illusionism is seen and reported through a delusionary or hallu-
cinated frame of reference. The following account from a Tsin dynasty
autobiography has that feeling, although most of the magic acts done
by the shamanesses can be reasonably accounted for.

His stepfather King Ning was sacrificing to his ancestors and had
engaged for this occasion two female wu [shamanesses], one Chang
Tan and one Ch'en Chu, who more than any others in the empire
were endowed with beauty. They were dressed very gaudily, and
chanted and danced excellently, and they could render themselves
invisible. The first evening was opened by them with bells and
drums, the noise of which they alternated with music of stringed
instruments and bamboo pipes, and then Tan and Chu drew knives
or swords, cut their tongues therewith, swallowed the swords, and
spat fire, a cloud hiding them from view, from which streams of
light flashed like lightning. . . . No sooner had [T'ung] entered the
door than he saw Tan and Chu in the central courtyard, dancing
with light steps and whirling round and round; they uttered a language of spirits and laughed like spectres, caused basins to spin and
fly against each other, and with gestures as though flying invited
one another to drink. T'ung stood horror-stricken; off he ran, not
through the gate, but right through the fence, and went home.

(de Groot, 1213)

The shamanism of this story represents a late stage of its development. Still, it suggests that delusionary or hallucinatory experience
remained an active aspect of shamanist performance. These modes may
be considered basic aspects of primal theatre, and an anthropological
sequence is then established in regard to a change in the perception of
illusion and deception, of illusion and reality, concerning a particular
modality of the "suspension of disbelief" in theatrical performance.

A particularly vivid example of the use of tricks and illusion as a
ground for delusionary experience is provided by Ronald Rose's
account of the phenomena that occur in Australian initiation rituals.
The candidates are secluded at night, and their nerves are worked upon

for a while by their initiators; a masked figure, which might be the god Baieme, approaches them and lies down:

> He lay on his back. His body gave a shiver and his mouth opened. Some of the men gasped almost inaudibly. From his mouth, the boys saw a thing come forth, a live thing that was not a snake, nor was it a cord. But it looked like a cord and moved like a snake. Slowly it issued from the gaping, quivering jaws, the length of a man's finger but not so thick. It moved about on the man's face and became longer, almost as long as a man's arm. It left his mouth and crawled in the grass. Then it returned to the man's body.
>
> (Rose, 103–4)

Later in the rituals, the adepts in magic, known as "clever-men," put on a display of rope tricks and illusionary acts:

> Clever-men appeared to lie on their backs and clever-ropes exuded from their mouths, their navels. The cords seemed to rise into the air, and the old fellows climbed hand-over-hand up them to treetop height. Then some of them moved from the top of one tree to the top of another by means of the cords, which swayed out into space. The boy had been told that clever-men could travel vast distances in no time with the aid of such cords; now he was seeing for himself some of these marvelous things.
>
> Some of the doctors walked straight to the trunks of big eucalyptus trees and appeared to melt into them, reappearing a moment later on the other side. (Rose, 104–5)

The boys are carefully prepared to be susceptible to the stimuli and suggestions of the ritual. A quartz crystal is used to hypnotize them or to deepen them in that state. It is difficult to tell how much is trickery and illusion and how much is delusion and hallucination. The magicians who walk through trees probably do no more than step around them, and suggestion does the rest. The basis for the "clever-ropes" is more difficut to perceive. Perhaps the shamans climb actual ropes into the trees, but most of the experience is clearly delusionary. Rose was shown such a cord in the presence of an aborigine friend who believed that he saw it, while Rose saw nothing on the demonstrator's first effort, and the second consisted of carefully drawing a string of saliva out to the length of a few inches. Some of the accounts in his study suggest that phenomena are reported as occurring if in some way they can be conceived of as happening. That is, the delusion may be conceptual, accepting the symbolic meaning of the trick, rather than perceptual. Any "sign" of a phenomenon is its manifestation. But there is a continuum of experience from delusion to hallucination, and the former is used to prepare the initiates for the latter.

Another paratheatrical performance originating in shamanism is represented by fire-walking, fire-handling, and fire-eating, typical of the type of act once practiced on street corners, in fairs, carnivals, and circuses in the Western world. In this category of performance, illusionistic trickery is combined with actual danger. It is so widespread and so characteristic of shamanism that Eliade considers a "mastery over fire" to be its "particular magic specialty" (Eliade, 5). One fundamental, cross-cultural source for these phenomena is a shamanistic trance ritual of exorcism held at night about a glowing fire. The !Kung Bushmen hurl burning brands into the darkness while shouting for the evil spirits to go away. The trance leads to paroxysms in which participants rush into the fire and scoop up hot coals, which they pour over themselves, singeing eyebrows and eyelashes and setting the hair on fire, and they scatter them over the spectators (R. Lee [S], 42; Marshall, 376–77). Ceylonese exorcism rituals are based on ecstatic dancing with lighted torches, which are rubbed on the dancers' bodies, placed beneath their garments without igniting them, and put into their mouths (Halverson: 338–39). Iroquois trance performers in masks scoop up and "juggle" live coals in their bare hands and scatter them upon spectators (Blau, 568). The pseudo-shamanism of the Shona of South Africa shows fire-handling as one specialization within a structured differentiation of shamanist ritual. Some of the practitioners "speak in foreign tongues, others are ventriloquists, and others again impress their clients by holding burning logs in their hands or live coals in their mouths" (Gelfand, 106).

There is some possibility that the nature of trance protects the participants in such acts, at least to some degree, from pain and injury. It must also do so in the acts of self-torture, which characterize much of Chinese mediumship, and is found in that of India, where it lies at the origins of the pseudo-shamanistic fakirism, with its beds of spikes. The Indian trance medium scourges himself with various whips, pierces his cheeks and tongue with a needle and his body with many small, decorated hooks, and he hangs suspended from a hook through his flesh (Rahmann, 736; Arasaratnam, 16–17). The Chinese shaman seats himself on a chair of swords, wounds himself with a sword or prick ball, pierces his tongue with a needle, and thrusts small ceremonial daggers through his flesh. The blood is absorbed by prayer papers, to give them efficacy, and these are distributed to worshipers (de Groot, 1275–79; Elliott; Jordan). The Moslem Darvishes place glowing coals and irons in their mouths and wound themselves with iron instruments which have been heated red-hot (J. Brown, 281). These performances might seem to represent an aesthetic which is at the oppposite pole from illusionism in which similarly gruesome acts are represented by trickery. They insist upon the virtuality of the body and of reality, forcing them to produce a sanctification of the trance. Like illusionism, they are demonstrations of the supernatural, of the transcendent, and like it they hold the virtual to be more real then ordinary reality. This, too, must be considered in regard to theories which hold that theatre originates in or is defined by imitation. Perhaps in shamanic self-torture we have spectacle as antitheatre, but it remains spectacle, a fundamental aspect of theatricality. The Chinese refer to the performances of their mediums with "a word of vigorous approval associated with an atmosphere of carnival and noisy confusion." It is difficult to say, however, that the self-torture of the medium is truly enjoyed. "Enthusiasm at a distance turns to morbid curiosity in face of the real thing, and the mob packs thick about the fenced-off court before the temple to watch the performance with profoundly involved but expressionless faces" (Jordan, 82). The aesthetics of trance performance, as such, place it close to self-torture in the sense that trance separates itself from reality so as to be the ground of reality, manifesting as the more real.

The illustionistic performances of the shaman's seance exact a tremendous psychological and physical price—which not everyone is prepared to pay—as does the "call" to shamanism.

In those regions where shamanism proper flourishes the only requirement for the call is the proper tendency to neurotic ecstasy and trance. The shaman need be neither pure in mind nor humble in spirit. All that is demanded of him is that he suffer physically. Many youths among the Chukchee, for instance, prefer death to the call of the spirits, according to Bogoras. The physical hardships and the mental suffering are too intense. Bogoras states that the process of gathering inspiration is so painful to young shamans because of their mental struggle against the call, that they are sometimes said literally to sweat blood on the forehead and temples. And after they have accepted the call, the spirits demand from them the impossible, such as showing no signs of fatigue after having been made to dance violently for long periods of time. At other times the spirits "play" with them, as they euphemistically say.

(Radin [P] : 161)

There is also some element of danger in acrobatic performances, and these appear to have had their origin in the trance dances of shamanistic exorcism ritual. Exorcism trance dances are a primal mode of shamanistic theatre, often treating the ills of the community, such as threats of plague or famine, and extending the trance from the shaman to the adepts who perform. Acrobatics and related skills such as jugglery develop in this context, apparently because heightened demands are placed upon the body and it is driven beyond its natural limits. The heightening of ability in dancing associated with trance possession has been observed in voodoo: "Spurred on by the god within him, the devotee who a few moments earlier was dancing without gusto, throws himself into a series of brilliant improvisations and shows a suppleness, a grace and imagination which often did not seem possible" (Métraux, 189). In the seance, the shaman often seems to be seized, shaken, and propelled by an alien force, "hurled to and fro, as it were in the grip of powers unseen" (Firth, 201). The somersault, characteristic of Western "ground" or "carpet" acrobats, is a symptom of the sudden onset of trance, as distinguished from the gradual onset, in the dance of the !Kung Bushmen (R. Lee[T], 31). Somersaults, spinning, jugglery, and other acrobatics are manifest in the trance skills of the devil dancers of Ceylon.

The dancing grows wilder and more furious, accompanied by the rolling of the drums, and the the throwing up and catching again of the torches. The torches are also flung to and fro among the dancers. Soon, the dance takes the form of wild leaps, and shakes, turns, and whirls of the head, the arms, the hands, and, finally, of the whole body. Now and then, one or the other of them will throw himself to the ground, only to jump up immediately, and other similar acrobatic feats follow each other with great rapidity.

(Wirz, 52–53)

Similar trance dances are widely practiced throughout Africa and may be said to be perhaps the most significant mode of the performing arts of that continent. Among the Tonga of Zambia, the majority of dances of the mediumistic society "no matter how sedate, climax in a period of violent action . . . the feet moving at incredible speeds, arms shaking, head shaking, whole body in vibrant motion," and we note again the effect of trance driving the body toward acrobatic action in a dancer who "finally falls to the ground and rolls about with great abandon, swings heels over head, goes rigid, with the body a curve supported only by heels and crown of head" (Colson, 87). In Nigeria, acrobatic dance is a feature of the masquerades.

> The dancer jumps up vertically and at the same instant twists in such a manner that he spins in the air in a near-horizontal position; so that, taking off on a left foot, he lands on a right a pace or two in advance of his starting point. Expert exponents of the *pegele* dance can be spectacularly acrobatic, moving across the arena in a flash, their bodies appearing to float across the air in a horizontal spin.
>
> (Alagoa, 153–54)

A similar horizontal spin is one of the movements that characterizes the acrobatics in Chinese theatre, and this association with trance dancing will be one of the means we will use to identify its origins. Codification and stylization of convulsive trance movements seem to have led to the various stands, leaps, and types of somersault of the ground acrobat. Arab acrobats, for example, have their own distinctive style, specializing in side leaps, leaps on one hand, and a twirling that "gives the impression of a spinning top motivated by the lash of a schoolboy." Strehly describes the "diabolical zest" with which the whole troupe performs simultaneously, encouraged by their own stamping feet and clapping hands, a "veritable wild music, which stifles even the sound of the orchestra under their deafening clamor" (Strehly, 287–8). The behavior in general and the spinning dance in particular seem to relate Arab acrobatics to antecedent ecstatic performances, such as those of the whirling Dervishes.

Another type of paratheatrical performance, puppetry, appears to originate as an aspect of the magical and supernatural aesthetic of shamanistic drama. Puppets are used in various ways by the shaman, particularly as "miraculous" extensions of the functions of divination and the giving of oracles. De Groot relates the story of a ninth-century Chinese shaman who created a puppet which then spoke with the voice of the spirit who was plaguing the patient, an effect undoubtedly achieved by ventriloquism (de Groot, 1,100). The Eskimo had "temporary images made of wood or stuffed skins" which would become possessed by a spirit, as well as stone images and wooden puppets that were used in divination (Lantis, 79). In Java, a puppet is put in a trance, as it were, by a mirror held before it—a common practice with human shamans. It begins to "twitch convulsively, like a human being entering into a trance," and then divines, with movements of the head answering questions posed to it (Epton [T], 118–19). Several types of puppet are used in this way as extensions of the shamanic functions.

> In Java, it was customary to construct a doll out of a dipper and a rice-steaming basket which was, by various measures, caused to be imbued with the spirit inhabiting a sacred site. Once animated, this puppet was able to dance and to give signs in answer to questions put to it, as a clairvoyant. In Bali, the *sanghyang déling* performance was a related development. Here two wooden puppets, on a string passed through a hole in their middles, would dance through the power of the spirits imbuing them. . . . At temple festivals, "heavenly nymphs" (*widiadari*) would be invited to descend as guests at the feast, to be embodied in little palm-leaf puppets (*gegaloeh*) made for the purpose. They would often be made to execute a dance, held in the arms of little girls or women who were said to "nurse" them.   (Belo [T], 12)

In New Britain, men carried on platforms by singing and dancing crowds in their festivals "manipulate carved and painted wooden figures or tricky props of other sorts involving sleight of hand for the mystification of onlookers. The spirits of dead kinsmen are called to stay in these objects during performance" (Valentine, 175). The Menominee shaman makes two small effigies dance by means of threads connected to his toes, demonstrating his magical power over them (Hoffman, 98), and the Malemute shaman uses a fetish with wolf body and alligatorlike head in his curing seances, causing it to move about beneath a parka and using ventriloquism to produce its growling. Shamanist puppetry reaches one of its points of highest development in the mechanical tableaux created by the Eskimos. Elaborate compositions of miniature figures were made to move; paddlers in kayaks, animals moving in and out of their burrows or holes in the ice, and birds that flapped their wings or descended by means of strings (Lantis, 69–72).

Similar techniques were used by the Kwakiutl in their winter spectacles of shamanic death and return from death, with wooden images operated by men on the roof and in tunnels beneath the ground, resulting in a magical abstract theatre that was a kind of life-sized puppetry. In one scene the initiate danced while a wooden image of a horned serpent rose from the ground and a wooden bird descended, guided by strings. In another scene, a wooden bird descends and appears to pierce the dancer's wrist with its beak; then a great rattle comes down from the roof, and a huge hand rises from beneath the ground, grasps the rattle, and shakes it (Curtis, 211–12).

Another trick of this kind is to have a wooden image of a man rise from the ground and an eagle descend from the roof and carry it away. Still another is that in which a box stands behind the singers, just high enough to be seen by the spectators. Water is poured into it, the initiate makes gestures toward it, uttering her cries, and presently a wooden loon bobs to the surface. It dives, and reappears. This happens four times. Then the woman calls for an eagle-tail, and with it she makes motions over the box, when a cloud of eagle-down flies upward. This is managed by a man who, concealed behind the singers, controls the wooden loon with strings running through the bottom of the box. After the loon trick is performed, he draws a plug, and the water runs into a pit and sinks into the ground. Through a hole in the side of the box is inserted the neck of a seal-bladder filled with eagle-down. He presses the bladder between his knees and the feathers fly upward. The uninitiated believe that they issue from the water.

(Curtis, 211)

The aesthetic of such scenes has much in common with that of the miraculous as represented on the Western stage, such as the descent of Renaissance "glories," clouds containing people. In general, puppetry continued to be performed alongside the other protodramatic arts in a kind of pseudo-shamanism, as in the masquerades of Africa or in the collection of acrobatics, magic, divination, fire-eating, and similar circuslike acts known as *saragaku* in Japan, which had their origin in ancient China. They are an important part of the great differentiation of shamanism into modes of secular entertainment as such, as if shamanistic ritual was the "great unitarian artwork" that fragmented into a number of performance arts, much as Wagner believed had been the case with ancient Greek tragedy. Fox gives an interesting account from Kilton Stewart's study of the *negritos* in northern Luzon (Philippines), which shows that this concept of shamanistic ritual as the "great unitarian artwork" is something more than metaphorical.

> Here the shaman induces a trance in the patient and instructs him to fight and overcome the "demon" that is attacking him and causing the complaint. Having mastered the demon, the patient demands from him a dance and a song. The shaman then ends the trance, and the patient is told to perform the dance and sing the song just learned—while the whole band witnesses the performance. The important thing about this type of cure is that all the aesthetic life of the band is derived from it. That is, all the songs and dances of the *negritos* are originally learned in such therapeutic trance conditions. These songs and dances are then regularly performed before the whole band, each person doing a dance-drama, in which he illustrates how he overcame his illness (the demon), and receiving the support and applause of the band. . . . A large slice of the total culture—the aesthetic and recreational—is involved, indeed is derived, from the therapy.   (Fox, 256)

The fundamental relationship of shamanism to the performing arts of a primitive culture is most often established by its relationship to the dream and to the dreamlike psychotic episode which there lie at the source of creativity. Contact with ghosts or spirits who "give" new masks, songs, or dances when they are encountered in the bush or forest is the source of creativity in New Guinea as in North America. Fugue states accompanied by hallucination are often recorded in terms of the origin myths for performances or masks. Such supernatural occurrences were the basis for the "vision quest" prevalent throughout North America, in which the seeker was given magic songs and ritual which, in effect, defined him for his lifetime. Particularly strong experiences of this type characterize shamanic initiation, establishing a pre-eminence in regard to the spirit-given creativity, so that often only the experiences of the shaman in trance or dreams are considered strong enough to provide the mask images or rhythms for the tribal performances. The winter ceremonies of the Iroquois center upon the shamanistic False Face Society and are characterized by performances in which the participants act out the particularly strong dreams they have had.

In trying to describe the special veracity given to masks by the relationship to spirits, it is often said that the mask *is* the spirit. This is intentionally redundant, but is somewhat inaccurate in regard to representation. The mask receives the presence and takes on the functions of the spirit. The basic relationship of the mask is to trance possession as an actualizer of its spirit. Many basic conventions of style in representing the face in African masks derive from the appearance of the face in trance (Thompson, 126ff.). When a Tlingit shaman of the northwest coast puts on his mask, "it is believed that he becomes possessed by the spirit represented, and the utterances of the shaman are for the time being regarded as the words of the spirit" (Stewart, 327). The same is true with the Kachina impersonators of the American Southwest and with the Lenape in the East (Stewart, 321–22). The masks of the Mandinka of the Gambia region of Africa have "the power to see in the past, present, and future–the ability to perceive evil, to identify sorcerers or witches, to detect the presence of spirits" (Weil, 282). These are the powers of the trance medium. To the Mandinka culture this power "is a parallel to spirit possession," and the "masker is not animated by his own will" (Weil, 283).

The basic concept of the mask seems to be associated with the use of body paint or elaborated costume which transforms the wearer into an animated sculptural figure. As noted, such figures are essentially abstract. One function of this abstraction is to create a disjunction with ordinary visual reality, a disjunction which is similar to that presented by the trance state itself. Like the spirit possession of puppets, the trance relationship to actual statues suggests the relationship of trance to performance by "animated sculptural figures." In China, the statue of the deity that possesses the medium is carried behind him in processions, seated in a sedan chair like a person. In Tibet, a huge figure of the goddess Lhamo on a massive structure is carried by men its spirit possesses.

> The chief actors on such occasions are the "sorcerers," who wear no masks themselves, but have the same type of hat and costume, bedecked with symbols, as is worn by the image of the deity. These "sorcerers" are basically the same as shamans; they not only represent the god and identify themselves with him, but are possessed by him and are the medium through which he speaks.
>
> (Lommel [M], 97)

The masked "sculptural figure" is directly identified with what is undoubtedly the most instrumental phase in the evolution of shamanistic theatre. The costumed personification of spirits, particularly of demons, is associated both with shamanistic ritual and with the dramas that then develop from these rituals. As a generalized category, such rituals and performances may be termed "demon plays." The Kwakiutl winter ceremony is essentially one long demon play. In Asia, we may observe ritual exorcisms which appear archetypal of the demon play's development into drama. One important kind is represented by the *cham*, characteristic of the Mongolian-Tibetan area, where Buddhist Lamaism is pervaded by the practices of an antecedent Bon shamanism. Waddell's account of the *cham* in Tibet draws heavily upon E. F. Knight's description of 1893 and presents a vivid picture of this exorcistic spectacle.

At a signal from the cymbals the large trumpets (eight or ten feet long) and the other instruments, pipes and drums, etc., and shrill whistling (with fingers in the mouth), produce a deafening din to summon the noxious demons and the enemies. "The music became fast and furious, and troop after troop of different masks rushed on, some beating wooden tambourines, others swelling the din with rattles and bells. All of these masks were horrible, and the malice of infernal beings was well expressed on some of them. As they danced to the wild music with strange steps and gesticulations, they howled in savage chorus. . . . The variously masked figures of Spirits of Evil flocked in, troop after troop—oxen-headed and serpent-headed devils; three-eyed monsters with projecting fangs, their heads crowned with tiaras of human skulls; Lāmas painted and masked to represent skeletons; dragon-faced fiends, naked save for tiger-skins about their loins, and many others. . . . but no sooner did these [priests] exorcise one hideous band than other crowds came shrieking on. It was a hopeless conflict.   (Waddell: 524–25).

The impression is of a continuous flow of action, but the *cham* is actually a "compartmentalized" sequence of scenes and does not enact an overall dramatic or symbolized narrative. In the Mongolian *cham*, for example, the action seems somewhat more formalized, and this compartmentalization is clearly apparent. There the performers use a single passageway out of which the different groups are summoned in turn by the weird and cacophonous music of an orchestra of cymbals, horns, and flutes made of human thigh bones.

Out of the gateway for the maskers, a pair of Gugor demons came into the arena. One of them wore a white mask with an angry expression and the other wore a plain white mask. They were accompanied by two skeletons, an old man with eight masked boys, two musicians playing the maskers' entrance music, two monks carrying censers, and one monk who showed the maskers the way.

The two Gugor dancers, who personified the Guardians of Knowledge, chanted mystical incantations (the Kalarupa). Through the patterns of their dance they called upon the fiends and spirits to spare their land from destruction. Concluding their dance, the Gugor left the arena.   (Forman and Rintschen, 111–12)

The *cham* of Nepal, which appears to be essentially identical with that of Mongolia, is a sequence of thirteen scenes of this type. "However, most of the presentations could be placed anywhere among the thirteen acts without disturbing the sense or purpose of the presentation. The only thread which connects the individual dances is a religious idea, the manifestation of good overcoming evil" (Jerstad, 107). We may consider this compartmentalized structure, a series of ritualistic dances, to be archetypal of the demon play as characteristic of a particular and important phase in the evolution of theatre. The origins of a theatre as we know it are to be found in the techniques by means of which the separate dances or acts are given an overall narrative, dramatic unity.

Stylistic similiarity with the Tibetan masks as well as a compartmentalized structure strongly suggest that Japanese *gigaku* and *bugaku* performances were originally exorcistic spectacles of the demon play type. Gigaku, formed from Chinese and Korean sources in the sixth and early seventh centuries, "comprised dances and pantomimes by performers wearing large skull masks to the accompaniment of music provided by a transverse flute, hip drums, and brass cymbals" (Araki, 36). A procession culminated in a ritualistic dance, "The Lions of the Five Directions," featuring the two-man lion figure common in exorcism throughout Asia, and this was followed by a series of masked solo dances and pantomimic numbers. In *Konron*, a six-character dance-drama, a lascivious phallic demon was subjugated, and other pantomimes were comic satires expressive of Buddhist moralization.

The two-man lion was used by itinerant shamanistic acrobatic troupes, and may be seen to this day in the Chinese circus performing an amazing dance on top of a huge ball. "The lion-dancers first ap-

peared in China under the T'ang dynasty (A.D. 618–906), and made
their début at the court of the kings of Tibet about the same time"
(Laufer, 29). In Tibet it performed such acts as dancing on a table
(Waddell, 539), and it is almost certainly the lion-dragon *barong ketet*
of Bali, although here there are also other animal-dragon *barongs*, such
as the pig *barong* and tiger *barong*, and *barongs* which are tall figures
worn by single performers. There are priests for each of the various
barongs, which are used in exorcisms, and they are operated by
performers in trance.

In the *Tjalonarang* exorcistic demon play, the benevolent *barong
ketet* has been brought into confrontation with another masked "sculptural figure," the disease-spreading witch Rangda, also acted by a performer in trance. The Rangda has a demon mask with protruding fangs,
large wig, massive costume, and long fingernails. A group of trance
dancers armed with krises attack the Rangda. They are thrown to the
ground again and again by the invisible emanations of her power, and
when they reach her they cannot kill her. They turn the krises against
their own bodies and dance convulsively with the movement of
stabbing suspended or "locked" by the trance, often bending the blades
of the krises against themselves. A group of women trancers also dance
in this way, and there are several comic skits which relate to the theme
of the play. The structure of the play is still essentially compartmentalized, composed of a number of independent scenes or events,
but it is given dramatic unity by the confrontation of the *barong* and
Rangda and by the relation of the performance to the myth on which it
is based, even though it does not use dialogue.

Ceylon provides a fourth area, with Bali, Tibet, and China and Japan,
in which we may observe the development of a demon play. The Ceylonese *sanniyakuma*, a ritual curing ceremony, begins in the evening and
lasts until the next morning. Much of the action is comprised of "devil
dancing," the spectacular acrobatic trance-dancing with lighted torches.
The main event, which occurs about midnight, is called the *pelapaliya*,
"the series of spectacles of the eighteen [demons]." The appearance of
each masked demon is preceded by a song recounting his life and death
and is announced by a crescendo of drumming. Each demon participates in a particular ritual, such as the spectacle of the shawls, the
spectacle of the torches, the spectacle of the sticks, and so on. The
demon or *yakka* converses with the head drummer or with one of the
other drummers, often in lengthy dialogues. As in the Siberian seance,

2. The demon Aimana in the Ceylonese *sanniyakuma* demon play. The painted face and false fangs relate such portrayals to the *vidusaka* clown in developed drama.

the demons ask presents as the price for halting their affliction of the patient.

Yakka: "What is going on here? What does this noise mean, gurunānsē?"
Drummer: "Somebody has fallen ill."
Yakka: "What are you going to do about it?"
Drummer: "We will give him a medicine."
Yakka: "That will not be of any use! There is no point in it! Give me twelve presents and I will cure him. But I must have my reward."

(Wirz, 53)

The shamanistic priests also carry on dialogues with the patient while he is in a state of spirit possession. If this does not happen spontaneously, an arrow is placed on the patient's head, apparently as a kind of lightning rod or conductor for the descent of the demonic spirit, and trance is induced by incantations chanted over him. The patient, his voice altered, then speaks with the voice of the demon, and the exorcist bargains with it, threatens, and tries other means to get it to leave the patient.

Priest: Tell me, what demon has possessed you?
Demon: Maha Sohonā has possessed me. I am Maha Sohonā.
Priest: Why do you cause harm to this human being?
Demon: He ate a certain kind of food without giving me my share of it.
Priest: We are prepared to give you an offering if you will leave the patient.
Demon: I want a human victim . . .

(Sharathchandra, 32)

Shock effect is often used in the attempt to cure the patient. His view of the ceremony is blocked out by white cloth curtains hung before him.

A demon wearing a black jacket, black "coat" and "trousers," black hat, his face and arms all coated with soot, enters the arena hooting and shrieking. He dances for a while and suddenly without warning throws apart the white curtain (kadaturāva) that had separated the patient from the preceding events and jumps at the patient as if to devour him. The patient gets a sudden shock; sometimes he shouts in alarm and always a startled reaction takes place. Even the audience is startled and there is a brief spell of silence. *Aturu Yaka* departs as suddenly as he arrived. (Obeyeskere, 188)

The plot of the *sanniyakuma*, elaborated in terms of dialogue, centers upon the attempts to get the demons to leave the patient. This must be considered an active, continuous process, like that of narrative dramatic form. Yet the *sanniyakuma* essentially remains another example of the compartmentalized, serial-scene structure characteristic of the demon play. However, it provides important clues which aid in the reconstruction of the development from the demon play of various folk plays in this area and thus of the probable origins of Sanskrit drama itself. But the *sanniyakuma* is in part already comedy. Let us first observe the evolution of the demon play into comic spectacles and consider its relationship to the origins of comic performance.

Clowning, as such, arises from a differentiation of the shaman's function as well as from representation of an antagonistic reality based on portrayal of spirits or demons of disease. One of the Zuñi clown societies, the Ne'wekwe, was a curing society, exercising the basic functions of the shaman (Parsons and Beals, 494). Another, the Koshare, specialized in shamanistic fertility magic. It is thought that "curing was almost certainly a primary function" of clowns among the Yaqui and Mayo (Parsons and Beals, 506). Among the Plains Indians, the "contrary" was often both clown and shaman. Ojibwa contraries masqueraded in grotesque costumes and practiced exorcism as a cure of sickness, particularly that caused by spirit possession, and the Canadian Dakota "consider the clown to be the most powerful of shamans" (V. Ray, 84–86).

Primordial clowning is everywhere associated with the irrational and with the demonic. The shamanistic clown societies of the Southwest are sacred because they are associated with the antiworld, an anarchy identified with death which is opposed to the order established and maintained in ceremonies by the benevolent masked gods. One of the clowns' primary ceremonial functions is to parody the dances of these masked gods while they are in progress. The grotesque costumes of clowns manifest this identification with the demonic.

The typical Koshare costume is that of the cadaverous-looking creature who represents death or the spirits of those dead: ancestors whom Indians call the Ancients. The effect is achieved by smearing bodies, faces, even hair with white clay, and painting the body with black stripes to suggest a skeleton. The head-dress of dried corn-husks and the rabbit skins around the neck symbolize death, and sprigs of evergreen tied to the arms mean recurrent life.

(Fergusson, 657)

These costumes are symbolic, rather than being intended for comic effect. Most often, they are awe-inspiring or frightening, rather than ludicrous. The Koshare clowns have been referred to as "these seeming monstrosities, frightful in their ugliness" (Bandelier, 134).

Among the Pomo and Patwin the clown was primarily an anti-natural being, a ghost, and the grotesque dress, strange behavior and contrary nature were as much an attempt actually to represent such a being as to produce a ludicrous impression. Moreover, within these tribes an atmosphere of sacred unnaturalness, even in regard to the buffoonery of the clowns, is attested by the fact that the audience was prohibited from laughing.   (Steward, 199–200)

In the differentiation of shamanizing in the Kwakiutl winter festival, the Fool Dancers' trance possession tends toward the comic, and they often attack others, as clowns can do elsewhere. "This possession causes excitability, madness, unnatural behavior, and it is provoked by the members of the opposing moiety" (Steward, 200). The Fool Dancers are represented with enormous noses, the striking of which drives them mad. They "personate fools and are characterized by their devotion to filth and disorder."

They do not dance, but go about shouting *wi. . . , wi. . . , wi. . . !* They are armed with clubs and stones, which they use upon any-thing that arouses their repugnance for beauty and order. Excreta are sometimes deposited in the houses, and the "fools" fling nasal mucus on one another.   (Curtis, 215–16)

One great paradox of clowning, which essentially manifests the anar-chic, insane, and demonic, is represented by the fact that the Kwakiutl fools, like the clowns of the Southwest, are charged with keeping order, watching over the behavior of others during the ceremonies. This relates to the critical function of the comic exercised as a social corrective. If the function of the comic is therapeutic, as well-known theories hold, we perceive one basic reason for the identification of clowning with the shaman, the society's doctor. The evolution of function is from treatment of physical ills caused by disease spirits, to the treatment of psychological ills caused by spirits, to a broader social application in terms of the comic-demonic.

It is this evolution which characterizes the development of the demon play into comic performance. The Ceylonese *sanniyakuma* was undoubtedly once an awesome spectacle, but the behavior and dialogue of the demons is now essentially comic. Obeyesekere has shown in detail how the demons were originally representations of physical illness but then came to portray the psychological meanings of symptoms and of psychosomatic and psychological illness in particular. One reason for this development would certainly be the realization, in the course of time and with the development of physical medicine, that shamanistic rituals achieve a higher percentage of cures with psychological illness than they do with physical illness. But essential, perhaps determining, characteristics of comedy seem also to have played a primary role in this transformation. The Ceylonese demon-clowns "express bizarre, psychotic thinking and sense confusion" because these are characteristics of the maladies they are treating (Obeyeskere, 202). A sense of strength and superiority is created in the patient and audience by demons who mock the sacred but are patently fools. The context, of course, is the actualized mysticism of the "devil dancing," and the element of fear plays an important part, as when the demon pounces suddenly upon the patient. The awesome, violent, and horrible aspects of the demon are first emphasized, but when he appears his behavior, except for his dancing, is comic. Obeyeskere observes that "these *inversions* not only ease the interaction situation, but prevent the attitudes one has towards demons in ordinary life from being generalized to the ritual situation" (Obeyesekere, 205). The comedy is functional, having some therapeutic effect, by making the symptoms laughable in terms of bizarre and psychotic behavior, and it also functions against psychological repression in general by acting out vulgarities that are not represented in sanctioned behavior.

The relationship to shamanism and to the demon play is illustrated by a primal phase of clowning in which the comic is identified with the representation of the diseased and deformed. Aztec comedies portrayed stupidity, drunkenness, madness, and deafness, and "farces about syphilis, colds, coughs, and eye complaints were presented in the temple of

Quetzalcoatl, who was believed to cause and cure these afflictions"
(Mace, 160). The six masked figures associated with the origins of the
Yoruba Egungun masquerade are a hunchback, an albino, a leper, an
individual with protruding teeth, a dwarf, and a cripple (Adedeji, 81).
In southern Nigeria, scrotal elephantiasis is considered a magical penalty
inflicted on adulterers, and thus is an object of laughter. The masks of
the *ekon* masquerades of the Nigerian Ibibio concentrate upon such
physical deformities related to ghosts.

> Traits condemned as ugly in songs sung at Ikot Ebak were the same
> (with the exception of protruding buttocks) as those carved and
> painted in *ekpo* masks to portray evil ghosts: swollen cheeks,
> bulging eyes, large ears, flat noses, sores of yaws and leprosy, swell-
> ings of elephantiasis, and black skin (members of *ekpo* when
> donning "ghost masks" blacken their bodies with yam charcoal to
> make them more ugly). Malformed genitals also figured in *ekon*
> satire.   (Messenger, 221)

Physical deformity, a source of the comic, is thus an aspect of spirit
possession. The origin of disease and other illness is ascribed by Iroquois mythology to the hunchbacked god Big Hump and his followers
the "false faces," "gangling creatures with large heads and distorted
features" who "are represented by the masked men who drive sickness
from the village every spring and autumn" (Müller, 192). Plains Indian
contraries are identified with grotesque mythological beings with anat-
omical distortions such as large, flapping ears or enormous mouths (V.
Ray, 103). Cherokee clowns called Boogers wear grotesque masks,
indulge in obscenity, and "distort their figures by stuffing abdomen,
buttocks, or shins." The humpback was a source of the comic in Aztec
performances, and it was characteristic of ancient Greek and Roman
mimes, as it was of the Turkish Karagoz, of Pulcinella, Punch, and other
Western comic types.

The physically grotesque distortion related to demonic representation
of disease and abnormality then becomes transposed into caricature of
social types and actions. In Malawi, undesirable character traits, such as
drunkenness or senility, are considered diseases caused by immoral
behavior and are represented in the twisted features of the masks
(Blackmun, 36). The face painting in Chinese drama shows it to be
derived from the demon-play exorcism, as we shall see, and the social
types who are represented with painted faces in the developed drama all

have something in their character that is deserving of criticism; that is, they are to some degree still demons. Strangers, either from neighboring tribes or as satirical caricatures of the white man, are subjects of comic representations in African masquerades as by the clowns of the American Indian. Foreigners manifest the quality of "otherness" associated with the demonic world, and that which is feared or hated on a social level is made comic. The personifications of social satire replace the demons in demon plays.

The otherwise awesome and impressive *cham* of Nepal includes two comic scenes, one in which an erroneous teacher of Buddhism is parodied in pantomime, and one in which a begging, itinerant Indian ascetic is caricatured. In Korea, the *sandae* mask play developed from a shamanistic base and is composed of ten independent scenes centering on individuals who are satirized, such as "The Pock-Marked Priest," "The Dark-Faced Priest," or "The Priest of the Blinking Eyes" (P. Lee, 84). The Korean mask play *Ha-Hoe* developed as part of a shamanist ritual and came to be composed of five satirical scenes; a young woman and a monk, a scene with four persons (nobleman, servant, scholar, concubine), an old lady and old man, a scene that represents two lions fighting (which is said to derive from exorcism), and the butchering of an ox played by an actor with a white cloth over him (Sang-Su). Social caricatures appear to have replaced demons.

The *kolam* folk play of Ceylon has been clearly derived from an exorcistic demon play of the *sanniyakuma* type and incorporates elements from other shamanistic rituals. It "is indebted to *several* ceremonies of the exorcistic kind for its characters and its masks," some of which "bear traces both of the influence of *bali* effigies as well as of Garā Yak masks" (Sarathchandra, 65–67). The *kolam* is performed throughout the night to the beating of drums in a setting like that of the *sanniyakuma*, a courtyard or arena in which a hut has been erected. Demon characters climb this hut, the *aile*, from behind and jump down in front of the audience, making a startling and dramatic entrance, as they do in the *Gara-yakuma* exorcism. A narrator describes the characters and announces their arrivals in verse, as in the *sanniyakuma*, with which some of the verses are identical. He also converses with them and sometimes interprets their actions to the audience. But much of the action is composed of a parade of mostly comic characters who appear one after the other, including a pregnant woman, a village woman, a European man and wife, a teacher, two bears, policemen speaking in broken English, a Moor, a Kaffir, and a moneylender. A drummer who appears as a character is represented as "a pot-bellied, hump-backed man suffering from elephantiasis" and is described by the narrator as "a skeleton with unkempt hair—a human decrepit" (Goonatilleka, 165). Two independent short plays are performed within the compartmentalized or serial structure, and it is significant that both are drawn from literature, and the one based on a Jataka story is approximately identical with the printed version. This shows the ability of demon-play technique to assimilate literature, a factor which will be important in tracing the origins of Sanskrit drama. The *kolam* includes a situation that provides a frame play for the action; a king and queen, played by the largest masks, watch the performance so that it will cure her of an illness. There is devil-dancing and an exorcism at the end, but the *kolam* is clearly a modification of demon-play curing, so that performance can be given as entertainment, as such.

Use of a narrator is a fundamental element in many of the folk plays of India, and the narrator in the *kolam* provides a significant clue to an explanation of their origins in shamanist ritual. The narrator or director of the performance, called the *sutradhara*, is also important in regard to Sanskrit drama.

Chapter II

INDIA: DEMON PLAY TO SANSKRIT DRAMA

The spectacular dance-dramas of South India have their origin in ancient Dravidian shamanism and its rituals of demon worship. In considering the process that created these plays, we may observe the influences which also shaped the basic forms of ancient Sanskrit drama. One type of dance-drama, *mudalapaya*, playing the characteristic stories from the *Ramayana*, is thought by some scholars to be typical of *prakrit* performances which influenced the Sanskrit drama (Ranganath, 68). *Kuttiyattam* is generally considered to be a remnant of that drama, passed on by a class of storytelling actor-dancers, descendants of the *sutas* of the ancient royal court. It is thought that *Krishna attam*, which developed about the middle of the seventeenth century, "is obviously a legacy of the exorcistic rituals of the devil dances and the rites of the Kali cult" (Singha and Massey, 86). Stylistic similarities allow us to reconstruct a general picture of the development of these dramas from antecedent, but still extant, trance rituals.

Ranganath feels that the dramas have taken their basic patterns from the *bhuta* ritual in which a number of men in "the traditional massive costumes" and armed with swords dance about the shamanistic medium costumed as a particular "ghost." He suggests that this presents "a highly similar picture to the court scene" in *yakshagana* drama and that the headdress and makeup characteristic of *yakshagana* derived from this source (Ranganath, 32–33). However, influence is actually more general than this single source implies. The headdress characteristic of South Indian dance-dramas is a tiered, somewhat conical crown, often backed by a halo, and the costume a full-sleeved blouse and long skirt that are often worn over padding. These derive from a traditional cere-monial costume of the shaman, such as that worn by the priests in Ceylon.

> On the appointed day, the dancing priest, who is termed Anumae-tirāla, and not Kapurāla (the ordinary title of a good-caste devil-priest), dons at the dēwāla the traditional dress of the god, consisting of a many-flounced coloured skirt or skirts, an orna-mental jacket with puffed out sleeves reaching to the elbows, and especially a tall tiara-like conical white hat (*toppiyama*), made in three tiers or sections, as well as a jingling anklet, *salamba* (in Tamil, *silampu*), and any other usual ornaments, bangles, etc., of his profession.   (Parker, 197)

In effect, this is the characteristic basic costume of the dance-dramas. Further elaboration of costume has been influenced by the demon enactments of shamanistic priests who wear huge, elegant costumes and massive headgear which often reach twenty feet in height. Over fifty demons are worshiped at different temples in Kanara alone, dedicated to glorification of the goddess Bhagavati (Karanth, 37). There are many types of trance ritual associated with the cult of Bhagavati, but the particular performance which is most clearly an antecedent of the drama is *Kaliyattam*, also called *mutiyettu* (crown wearing), which represents a battle between the demon-goddess Kali and the demon Darika. Performers in trance and wearing the huge costumes of Kali and Darika are carried standing on wooden litters by ecstatic crowds. "Shouts of defiance, dramatic dialogue, and challenging gestures of the goddess and her demon foe whip up the excitement of the crowd that moves along in the procession around the temple led by the drummers" (Devi, 123). The two then walk about enacting a combat in the temple area throughout the night until Kali kills Darika just at daybreak, "when it is neither day nor night." "The chief item of the murder scene is when *Kali* plunges her hands into the very bowels of *Darika* followed by the drinking of and besmearing the body with blood, and ultimately she adorns herself with his intestines" (Pisharoti, 171). The pattern of this ritual seems to have directly influenced the dance-dramas. In the *Prahlada Charitram* play performed in *Bhagavatha mela* style, Nara-

3. A medium of Bhagavati as Valia Tamburatti, the Great Goddess.

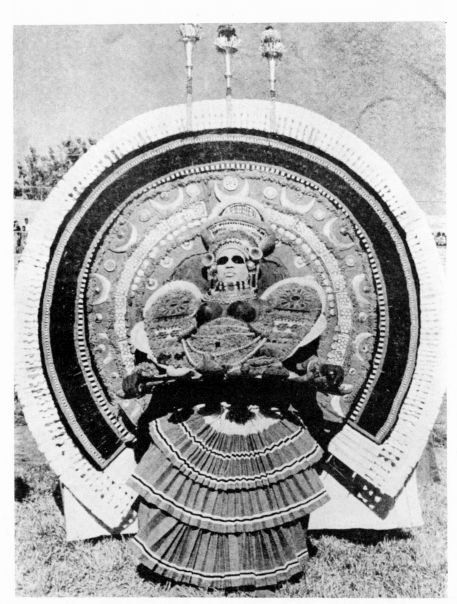

4. A medium as the goddess Kali in the Kaliyattam demon play of North Malabar, India.

5. A demonic, crown wearing figure of the ritualistic *kathakali* drama of India.

shimha, the man-lion incarnation of Vishnu, destroys the demon Hiran-
yakashipu in this way, and the actor playing the part often goes into a
trance (Gargi, 138). In the *kathakali* performance of the Dushasana
Vadha play, based on the *Mahabharata*, Bhima tears out the entrails of
the demonic Dushasana, concluding a battle that lasts one hour and
ends at daybreak (Devi, 89). A similar episode is also performed in the
therukoothu style, concluding a cycle of eight plays performed in
honor of Draupadi, but here the actor playing Bhima smashes a hollow
clay statue of Duryodhana from which a bloodlike liquid then flows
(Gargi, 136–37). Like the *Kaliyattam*, these dance-dramas start in the
evening and last all night, and they are based on battle scenes. A frequently encountered hypothesis that such battles somehow derive from
performance in military camps is certainly not credible; shamanism,
such as the costumed priests cited above who carry swords, everywhere
armed itself to battle demons in exorcism, and this is clearly the source
of the dramas.

A particular mode which appears in the dance-dramas and in related
types of performance includes monologue, monodrama in which one
actor plays several parts, and dances based on a series of poses. Acting
(*abhinaya*) in the classical dance styles is essentially a monologue de-
livered to an invisible or imaginary person, but this has occasionally led
to the representation of such persons by other performers. The solo
performance seems to be a unique characteristic of the drama of India,
and it appears to derive from the solo enactments and dances of
shamanistic spirit possession. In Burma, an announcer sings an ode
which recounts, in the first person, the life of the *nat* to be represented,
and the *nat-kadaw* medium dances dressed in a costume representing
her spirit-husband, chanting an ode in the person of the *nat*. The action
is defined by a combination of concepts or modes in which "the nat is
not only the spectator of and symbolically represented in the dance,
but is also the dancer. Although it is the shaman's body that is dancing,
it is the nat who is in fact performing the dance" for himself (Spiro,
120–21). The introductory verses recounting the life and death of the
nat are similar in content and technique to those sung before the entrance of the demons in the *sanniyakuma*. This would be the origin of
the verses which introduce the characters in the dance-dramas, such as
Bhagavatha mela or *kuttiyattam*, which describe the earlier life of the
character. In *kuttiyattam*, these verses, as shown by identical last lines,
"are therefore similar to the entrance *Dhruvā* of the Sanskrit dramas
prescribed in the *Nātyaśāstra*" (Raja, 13). The verses of introduction in

Bhagavata mela have also been identified with the Sanskrit *dhruvas* (C. Jones, 195).

In *kuttiyattam*, shamanistic monologue has become monodrama in which a single actor plays a number of characters in turn on all but the final night, on which a group of actors appears. And we can see that the linking technique, as in other dance-dramas, is the use of a narrator, the drummer in the *sanniyakuma* or the narrator for the *nat-kadaws*, who is the *sutradhara* in Sanskrit drama. "The actual *sūtradhāra* in Bhāgavata Mēla is the conductor of the drama and the musicians. He enters verbally into occasional scenes with the actors as the play progresses, afterwards returning to his function of conductor" (C. Jones, 195). It has been thought that the term *sutradhara* relates to an origin in puppetry, so that it would mean "holder of the strings" of the puppets, but it would clearly mean "holder of the thread" of the narrative, just as the narrator does in the *kolam* derived from the demon play. In *yakshagana*, "when the verse refers to a particular character on stage, that particular character alone keeps dancing in consonance with the mood of the verse" (Ranganath, 52). A thirteenth-century treatise describes *yakshaganas* danced by *devadasis* in which all the characters were portrayed by a single performer. *Kuchipudi* dance-drama contains a number of solo performances of this kind, such as one in which the dancer acts in turn Shiva, the demon-goddess Durga, and the demon Mahishasura.

> The dancer's swift transition to the role of the monstrous Mahish—Durga's powerful challenge—and the battle dance, alternating the roles of the two combatants (danced to *sabdas* accented on drums) carries the dramatic sequence to the supreme climax—the final victory of Goddess Durga, worshipped (in a still pose) with chants of praise and waving of lighted lamps.   (Devi: 75)

Such enactments, as well as solo sequential representations, appear to have originated in the concept of "serial possession," a very usual type of seance, in which the medium incarnates many spirits in succession and speaks and acts for each. The *sanniyakuma* appears to have originated in the use of masks to theatricalize serial possession. With the information then at his disposal, Pertold hypothesized that it had originated in the performance of a single medium who wore the eighteen masks in turn, and Lommel refers to a Ceylonese curing ritual in which masks are worn in sequence by the shaman (Lommel [M], 84). Quite probably the *dasavatara* sequence in *Kuchipudi* drama, where the ten avatars of Vishnu are represented by song and actions which culminate in symbolic still poses, had an origin in this phenomenon. *Orissi* dance also contains enactments of divinities in a sequence, with a descriptive Sanskrit *sloka* sung to accompany each, and the performer on conclusion falls into trance (Pattanaik, 38).

Another characteristic feature which relates the dance-dramas to antecedent ritual is the "curtain look" used for the first entrance of principal characters in *Kuchipudi, Bhagavata mela, kathakali, therukoothu*, and *yakshagana*. The character remains partially hidden by a hand-held curtain, while he howls, peers over the top, and dances, or he makes his appearance gradually, by lowering the curtain, building up the suspense of the entrance. The "curtain look" would certainly seem to have derived from the entrances of demons in rituals of the *garayakuma* and *sanniyakuma* type, and particularly from the effect in which the demon dances behind a curtain and then pulls it aside to pounce upon the patient.

A very significant characteristic of the dramas of South India is the use of a gesture code which can, as in the case of *kathakali*, approach the facility of a spoken language. It is found in *Bhagavata mela, Kuchipudi, kathakali, kuttiyattam*, and *Krishna attam*, as well as in *Orissi* dance, the *kathak* dance of North India, and in the dance of **Manipur** in the far eastern part of India, among other forms. Such a gesture code, in which the hand symbols are termed *hastas* or *mudras*, is identified with the now classical mode of the *devadasi* temple dancers. Codification of a gesture system of this type was given in the *Natyashastra*, the semisacred "fifth Veda" attributed to Bharata-muni, which presented a systematization of all aspects of the Sanskrit drama and is thought to have been written in the second or third century.

Mudras appear as hand poses in Buddhist iconography about the start of the Christian era and are then elaborated further in the iconography of Tantrism. Tantrism also developed the use of *mudras* in trance-inducing rituals which must have existed long before the fourth century. There the gestures accompany the saying of *mantras*, mystic sound poems, and are used to project the body of a divinity upon that of the worshiper. It is thought that the use of *mudras* "must go back to some ancient source closely connected with the primitive dance" which would seem to furnish "the prototype of the iconographic and ritual gestures of later times" (Saunders, 11). In that case, however, the dances, like the rituals that might have developed from them, were based upon spirit possession. This is apparent in the dance of the *devadasis* (servants of god) of Manipur, where male and female shamanistic mediums called *maibas* and *maibis* use the gestures to invoke or call down the gods who will possess them in trance.

> Now the Maibis (generally two) will dance and practice a few steps on the grassy lawn, before the village hut meant for housing the particular god or goddess. They would sit before the Lord and, trance-like, act as oracles to prophesy the fortunes of the village. . . . Then the Maibis would stand up and dance to welcome the gods, which is known as *Jagoi Okpa* (reception to the gods). Now the gods and goddesses respond to the call and they watch and play. Various Mudras like *Musti, Hamsasya* and *Ardha Chandra* will emerge from the delicate hands of the Maibis who dance now *Lai chingba* in elaborate movements. The gods and goddesses arrive at last. (Singh: 31)

An attempt has been made to associate the deities of Manipur with those of the Vedas, but however that may be, the function of the *devadasis* as trance mediums clearly reflects a very ancient tradition.

It seems probable that *mudra* gestures were first based upon a representation of ritual objects, such as the trident, conch, arrow, or lotus. We note that in Tantric iconography some hands of a deity make symbolic gestures while others hold ritual objects. This would relate the *mudras* to the pattern of shamanistic dances with ritual objects which is found throughout Asia, even though the latter practice would seem to have developed from iconography. The ritualistic *kagura* dance of Japan, originating in performances of the *miko* shamaness, is a hieratic honoring of ritual objects held by the dancer. Several of these ritual objects are identical with those carried in mediumistic dances by the *nat-kadaws* of Burma. The sword, bowl, fan, bead rosary, and the branch or twig of a tree are objects common to both types of dance. In Ceylon, the handling of ritual weapons by the shamanistic priest "appears conducive to possession" (Yalman, 128). The *mudras* used in rituals performed while seated by the Buddha priests and Shiva priests of Bali are clearly conducive to trancelike identification with a deity, while similar seated rituals of the Shingon sect of Japan are specifically directed toward trance possession and include *mudras* for various deities as well as a touching of ritual objects, such as lotus flowers, weapons, and the iconographic thunderbolt *vajra* (de Kleen, Epton).

6. Balinese exorcist using *mudra* gestures in a ritual to expell evil spirits while an assistant makes noise with a conch shell. Noise of a drum and a chime of bells, not shown here, also accompany the ritual.

The seated dance performed in *kathak* style, in which *mudras* and facial expressions are used to interpret a song of devotion, would seem to show the use by dance of the related rituals of this type. The whole codification of gesture, from *karana* poses to movements of various parts of the body, thus appears to originate in a fluid iconography devoted to hieratic manifestation of a deity possessing the dancer during trance, and a narrative ability in which gesture is used to interpret songs and dramatic passages then develops in scope from this basis. The gestures of the Shingon priest, which are called "seal bindings," are a gesture language directed to the spirits.

> To one seeing them for the first time, nothing appears so far out of this world: the controlled vehemence with which the "knots" are tied, the uncanny flexibility of the finger-joints (each one of which has a special name), the strange appearance of the knots themselves, the abandonment to the performer who appears to be possessed by finger-spirits. . . . With his fingers the *nakaza* calls upon the good spirits and expels the evil ones.   (Epton, 232)

This reconstruction of the origins of drama in India is verified by the *Natyashastra*. Bharata tells us that the first play, which was to be presented at Indra's Banner Festival, represented "an imitation of the situation in which the Daityas were defeated by gods [and], which represented [sometimes] an altercation and tumult and [sometimes] mutual cutting off and piercing [of limbs and bodies]" (I, 55–58; Ghosh, I, 9). The *Daityas* were demons, and the play would approximate a demon play of the *Kaliyattam* type, in which the demon Darika is disemboweled by the demon-goddess Kali. *Mudras* are used in ritual by the Bhagavati cult of South India. On an even more empirical level, the play would relate to exorcistic possession dances, such as those of Malabar, in which the shamanistic *Velichapad* priest gashes himself with a sword. Elaborate costumes and headgear are worn in this performance, the face is painted in striking designs, and "the toilet of decoration in [these] spirit dances is an elaborate and long process" (Raghavan, 54), just as it is in *kathakali* and other dance-dramas.

According to the *Natyashastra*, a difficulty then arose in the presentation of the first play to be performed. The demons who were present in the audience objected to the representation of their defeat, and "the Vighnas (evil spirits) together with the Asuras resorted to magical power and paralysed the speech, movement as well as memory of the actors" (I, 66; Ghosh, I, 11). The meaning of this would seem to be that the trance state, as practiced in the rituals which precede drama, places limitations on histrionic abilities. Indra resolved this situation at the performance of the first play when he took up his banner staff, the *jarjara*, and "smashed to pulp the Asuras and the Vighnas who were hanging about the stage" (I, 71–3; Ghosh, I, 11). The Vighnas continued "to create terror for the actor," so a playhouse was built, its various parts identified with various gods for protection, and "in the Jarjara was posted Thunder (*vajra*) the destroyer of the Daityas," and its sections were identified with the great gods (I, 76, 88–93). The first play as described in the *Natyashastra* is thus not really a drama but a demon play as exorcism. The narrative describes a transposition of the function of the banner staff from its uses in trance ritual to its uses in rituals which preceded a performance of Sanskrit drama, the practice of which is still found in *Kuchipudi* and *chaau* performances.

The *Natyashastra* says that the *jarjara* may be made from a tree or branch but is preferably made from bamboo. "[One should fasten a piece of] white cloth at the top, blue cloth at the Skanda joint, and variegated cloth at the lowest joint" (III,74–76; Ghosh, I, 41). The *jarjara* used in the preliminaries to *chaau* performances is described as "a red banner tied with mango leaves" and hoisted on a pole (Gargi, 168). The ritual function of the *jarjara* as a vertical "conductor" for possessing spirits, and hence as a "weapon" against disease demons, can be reconstructed from a number of sources. Shamans of the aboriginal Ceylonese Veddas tie two clusters of leaves to an arrow, "one just below the feathers and another immediately above the blade," and stick it into the ground as a means to possession. "The shaman afterwards explained that the *yaka* first came to the arrow and the leaves tied to it, and then entered the persons of the dancers who became possessed" (Seligmann, 216). In another possession dance, the Vedda shamans each carry two arrows which are the "conductors" for the possessing spirit (Seligmann, 159). I have noted the arrow placed on the head of the patient in the *sanniyakuma* to induce possession in this way. The possession dance of the primitive Paniyan hill tribe of Kerala appears similar to that of the Veddas; it takes place around an upright pole, and the dancers hold two sticks over their heads, undoubtedly to act as such "conductors" for the spirit (Raghavan, 51). In the shamanistic ritual which provides the context for the Korean *ha-hoe* mask play, the spirit descends through a pole three and a half feet long with a spirit bell on top, causing it to tremble and possessing the person who holds it (Sang-

Su). The Japanese Shingon priest who uses *mudras* is possessed by a spirit that descends through a *gohei* wand placed upright before him, causing it to tremble in his hands. The *gohei*, a decorated staff representing a tree or branch, is also carried by the *miko* shamaness in *kagura* dances, undoubtedly as such a "conductor" for the spirit. In Japanese *matsuri* festivals, the spirit descends a pine tree to possess a dancer who stands beneath it (Keene, 35). The branches carried in the dances of the Burmese *nat-kadaw* mediums relate to the trees with which the *nats*, their spirit-husbands, are identified, and also clearly function in this way. The center point of the stage in a Burmese theatre is marked with a tree, suggesting the origin of performance from shamanism. The exorcistic *cham* demon play of Nepal is performed around a thirty-foot-high banner-staff adorned with prayer flags, and similar poles are also found in Burma. They derive from the shamanistic Bon religion, and the ascent of prayers by means of the flags would then have replaced the ascent of the shaman's spirit along the vertical "road" of a tree or of a pole identified with a tree, the practice which is characteristic of Siberian shamanism. A winged horse is most often represented on the flags as carrying the prayers to the spiritual realm, and the Siberian shaman is thought of as riding a horse as "vehicle" on his trance travels.

In the Indonesian *wayang kulit* shadow play, the most important puppet is the *kayon* which combines the image of a tree with that of a mountain. It is set up at the beginning and end of the performance and is used in a number of symbolic ways throughout. Ascent of the "mystic mountain," like ascent of the tree, is a factor in Siberian shamanism; both represent the "axis mundi" along which the spirit moves in trance travel. The *kayon* is also set up before a performance of *wayang topeng*, a masked pantomime derived from *wayang kulit*, and the *dalang*, who narrates the performance and creates the voices for the dialogue of the actors, is most often still a *dukun*, a shaman (Onghokham, 114,121), so that we have good reason to believe both forms originated in shamanistic ritual. "Traditionally, the function of the shadow play is bound up with exorcism, propitiation and invocation of fertility" (Holt, 125). Originating in shamanistic exorcism, the demon figures of *wayang kulit* then took their place in the stories from the *Ramayana* which came to be represented. This would explain why they are often shown as opponents of the Pandawas, rather than the Kurawa opponents who figure in the stories (Brandon, 28). Claire Holt suggests that the *kayon* has a parallel and possible prototype in the *jarjara* (Holt, 135). She also suggests the most important key to the shamanistic

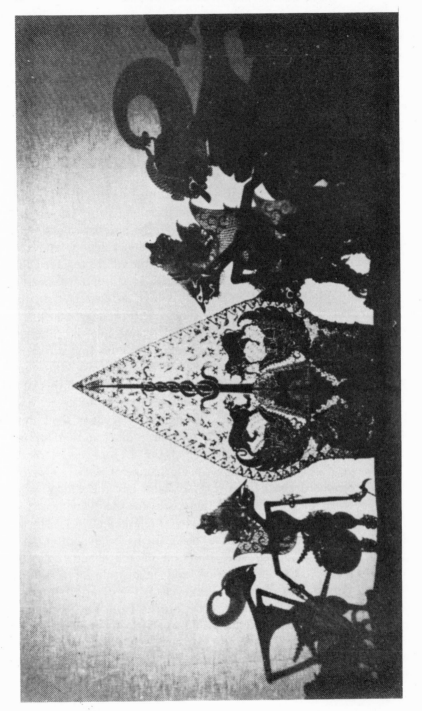

7. Balinese *wayang kulit* shadow play characters with *kayon*. Two snakes twine about the tree which forms the vertical axis.

origins of the drama of India and Indonesia, the similarity between the *dalang* and the *sutradhara*.

> There are striking parallels between the qualifications demanded of a dalang and those that were required, on the one hand, of the Indian *sutradhara*, director and producer of classical drama and, on the other, of a shaman who officiates today in a Dayak community of Central Borneo. (Holt, 132)

In northern Sumatra, the shaman does a solo dance with a *tunggal panaluan* or magic staff topped with fibers and sometimes planted in the ground, saluting it again and again, and talking to it (Holt [B], 67). In the cult of Bhagavati in South India, the spiritual presence of the demon-goddess is "symbolized by a branch of the sacred *pāla* tree and a *pītham* or the heavy ceremonial wooden stool covered over by a red silk cloth and a sword resting on the seat" (Ragahavan, 26). A possession dance occurs, and the enclosure within which these objects are placed is destroyed by the trancers. We have noted the carrying of a sword as characteristic of the possession dances of Bhagavati worship, and her symbolic branch is undoubtedly again the "conductor" in spirit possession, as with the *nat-kadaws*, rather than "indicating a definite cult of the tree," as Raghavan believes. James Frazer, from whose context such hypotheses proceed, was either not aware of, or did not care to mention, the use of the tree or pole as a "road" for trance flight in Siberian shamanism, preferring to represent the shamanic precinct as a "sacred grove" apparently dedicated to the worship of trees (Frazer, 108). In a similar manner, Raghavan relates the *kalasam* to the tree. Kalasams are structures for offerings carried on the head in Bhagavati worship, highly decorated and based on "a bamboo pole four to six feet in height with tiers of interlaced wood work narrowing in dimensions towards the top" (Raghavan, 28). Therefore it is suggested that we may "discern in the cult of the decorated pole another survival of tree cult, a cult which must once have been very vigorous in a land of hills and valleys, where the people lived as they still do, a simple life in harmony with nature" (Raghavan, 28). This adequately represents Frazerian reduction to the pleasantly banal, but it does considerable injustice to the price people have paid for the manifestations of the supernatural spiritual world. The *kalasam* more nearly relates to the *kavadi*, a structure for offerings carried on the head of a trance-walking penitent and "borne by a micro-distribution of a thousand elongated needles pressing upon the exposed chest and back and abdomen" of the bearer (Wavell, 148). Such structures are related to the treelike shape containing a pot full of water which is balanced on the head of a *katagam* dancer (Arasaratnam, 22) and to the decorated "water pitcher" carried on the head of a trancer possessed by an aspect of Kali in the preliminaries to *chaau* in which the *jarjara* is carried (Gargi, 168). The principle would clearly seem to be movement of the spirit in possession, and of the offerings, along the vertical axis represented.

The *devadasi* temple dancer was married to a deity, sometimes represented by a statue and sometimes by a tree, in a ceremony which included use of a sacred cord, just as does the marriage ritual of the Burmese *nat* shamaness, which also involves a eugenia branch. This suggests that the ancient *devadasis*, like the *nat*-wives, practiced spirit marriage. Further proof of this is given by the myth of Urvasi, the archetypal *apsara* or *devadasi*. It tells how the *devadasis* acquired the *talaikole*, "the earthly symbol of Indra's sacred banner-staff," the *jarjara*. Urvasi, dancing in Indra's court, was distracted for a moment when her gaze met that of Jayanta, Indra's son, and a curse was placed on them both by Agastya, the sage and patron saint of South India. Urvasi was forced to dance on earth as a *devadasi*, and when she made her debut she was presented with the *talaikole* which was her lover, Jayanta, represented in the form of a bamboo pole. Jayanta himself had been transformed into a bamboo tree growing in the mountains. But upon presentation of the *talaikole*, "both she and Jayanta were freed from the curse and ascended to the heavenly abode of Indra" (Devi, 45). The *talaikole*, the *devadasi's jarjara*, would clearly seem to be the staff associated with the tree as "conductor" in the union of the spirit with the possessed one in trance.

The verses used in the classical dances, such as *Bharatanatyam* and *kathak*, identified with the *devadasis*, often beg the god to come, and it seems most probable that this was at one time more than amorous and sexual invitation, and that it represented or derived from an invocation summoning spirit possession. The content of the verses was greatly affected by the ecstatic *bhakti* movement of the medieval period, so that they are now almost invariably identified with adoration of Krishna. But the basic form of the dances and the use of these verses must reflect much of the older tradition. The first verse given here is an invocation called *sabda*, a gesture song of praise to a deity or king, and the second is a *padam*, a gesture song usually on erotic themes.

O, Thou Lord Shiva, favoured of the Goddess of Fortune, Beautiful One, Destroyer of Enemies, praised at all times by the learned in the arts, Giver of Plenty to all—to Thee I bow.

When I wait for Thee, who alone art my guide, is it fair that Thou shouldst favour another with Thy presence?

O Great Lord, I tremble with love and devotion for Thee.

I cannot bear the flowery arrows on Manmatha, the God of Love—O, Thou with a third eye in the middle of the forehead, I seek Thy protection and bow to Thee.

Krishna Ni Vegame

Krishna, come quick and give a glimpse of the three worlds.
O Krishna of blue complexion, come dancing with anklets tinkling
  and pendants dangling.
With rings of Thy fingers, wearing a garland of Vyjayanthi, clad in
  yellow silk, with a flute in hand and with the body smeared with
  sandal, do come soon, O Krishna.
O Saviour of the world! O Krishna! do come and show the Universe
  in Thy mouth.   (*Classical and Folk Dances of India*, 25–60)

These verses may be compared with somewhat similar invocations to a deity of the opposite sex found in the shamanistic *Nine Songs* of China of the fourth century B. C. and understood to refer to spirit marriage. The myth of Urvasi, the relationship of *mudra* gestures to trance, and the shamanistic *devadasis* of Manipur are other elements in the pattern that make such a reading probable in regard to the ancient *devadasis*.

The first play, then, represented exorcism in which demons were driven off by use of the *jarjara* as vertical axis and "conductor" in trance possession. According to the *Natyashastra*, the second play ever produced was a representation of the hieratic cosmological event called "The Churning of the Ocean," associated with the tortoise avatar of Vishnu. The event itself seems to have been a mythological archetype of the trance state, portrayed by the churning, and of its various aspects or results, represented by the symbolic objects and persons produced by the churning. The ocean would symbolize the unconscious activated in trance, and the whirling motion of the churning suggests the vertigo of trance as well as spinning and circular modes of trance dance. The mountain used as a churning stick is essentially the "mystic mountain" found in Siberian shamanism, and the poison spit upon the demons by the serpent Vasuki who was used as a churning rope is an archetype of the function of trance curing as exorcism. That is, the basic image is that of an exorcistic demon play.

This interpretation is validated by the figure of the "physician of the gods" who is produced by the churning. The other entities thus produced relate to other aspects of trance phenomena. The celestial tree would symbolize the conductor used in spirit possession, and the divine horse would be the shaman's "vehicle," ridden to the sky world on his trance travels, as in Siberia. The goddess of fortune, Lakshmi, would represent one aspect of trance divination or curing, and the goddess of wine, Varuni, would symbolize intoxication as instrumental in trance or as a state related to trance. The celestial nymphs (*apsaras*) said to be produced by the churning are archetypes of the *devadasi* dancers. In Bali, little girl trance dancers called *sanghyangs* are thought to be possessed by the *apsaras* (Holt, 118). The royal elephant most probably represents royal sanction for trance, but other accounts mention more elephants, and in the Ceylonese *gam maduva* ceremony groups of men in trance enact a band of maddened elephants who "want to go to the god" (Yalman, 143, 146). The wish-cow, Surabhi, daughter of Ritual Skill and a seer, Vision (Danielou, 316), would then relate to the fanciful, hopeful, and wish-fulfilling aspects of trance ritual, divination, oracles, and curing. The celestial jewel would seem to relate to the profundity of mystic experience in trance or as associated with trance, and the conch is a musical instrument used in performance but is also of significance as a ritual object, and its structure might be a metaphysical representation of the churning. Thus "The Churning of the Ocean" is a multifaceted image of trance, the whole process being supported by Vishnu, the "ground" of being, in his tortoise incarnation as a base for the churning stick. In the Khmer version of the archetypal myth, the turning of the churning staff causes Vishnu to ascend from its base to its top, where Brahma is seated, an ascent of the vertical axis similar to that of the tree or pole in shamanic trance flight. The ocean itself, said to be of milk, is clearly a ritual entity and would relate to ceremony such as the Ceylonese *gam maduva*, in which a large pole known as the "milk-exuding tree" is erected (Yalman, 143). "Milk bowl" is the literal translation of the name of the pantomimic possession dance performed by the Veddas of Ceylon as hunting magic (Seligmann, 218). The second play as represented in the *Natyashastra* thus commemorates the generic origins of Indian drama.

Much of this same symbolism is represented in the elaborate costume of a trance medium, such as those associated with the Bhagavati cult of South India, as it is described in the *Silappadikaram*, which is thought to date from the second century. The costume is described twice, and this version may relate to a statue of the deity who possesses the medium, but it indicates the hieratic associations.

Just then, She who wore the moon in Her coiffure, she who had an unwinking eye in Her forehead, coral lips, white teeth, a throat darkened by poison, who had the serpent Vāsuki of unquenchable ire for Her girdle, and mount Mēru for Her shoulder-bangles, whose breasts were enclosed within a bodice resembling a serpent's venomous teeth, and who wore elephant hide for Her upper garment and a lion's (tiger's?) skin for Her petticoat, (appeared), with a trident [of Vishnu] in her bangled hands. Her left foot was adorned with *silambu* and the right with a victorious anklet. Skilled in sword-fighting, the Lady who stood on the head of the double-bodied broad-shouldered Asura [demon], the goddess worshipped by man, Kumari, Kavari, Śamari, the holder of the trident, She whose hue is blue, the younger sister of Vishnu the giver of victory, the holder of the cruel axe, Durgā, Lakṣmī, Sarasvatī, the image adorned with rare gems, the ever-youthful Kumari whom Vishnu and Brahmā came to worship, declared the form and attire of the divinity-possessed Kumari quite god-like.   (Dikshitar, 182–83)

The blue hue cited would appear to be an example of colors associated with representations of divinities which provided the basis for the system of painting the faces and limbs of actors in Sanskrit drama as described in the *Natyashastra*. We are told that Narayana (Vishnu) and Vasuki as well as the demons should be dark blue (XXIII, 92–93), and this system is extended to characters that are painted various colors in accord with "their place of action, and time of action, birth and the region of the earth they dwell in" (XXIII, 103–4; Ghosh, I, 426).

The circular trance dance symbolized by the Churning of the Ocean became a form of drama, the *raslila*, promulgated by the ecstatic *bhakti* (devotional) movement which began in the south in the thirteenth century and swept across Northern India in the fourteenth to seventeenth centuries. The concept of *ras*, the dance portion of *raslila*, was based on a legend in which Krishna first disappeared from among the *gopis* (shepherdesses) and then appeared again playing his flute in the middle of their dancing circle. His image then became multiple, so that there was a Krishna between every two *gopis* and each *gopi* was between two Krishnas. In *ras* dances, the sacred presence of Krishna is often represented by a lamp in the center of the dancing circle. In the *ras* performed in Madras, Vedic mantras are sung to transfer power to the lamp from lithographs of Radha and Krishna on the wall (Singer, 95). The lamp would be, in effect, a substitute for the pole as a source of the possessing spirit, as in the circular Paniyan or Vedda dances cited above. In the characteristic *raslila*, group possession takes place between the *ras*, in which young boys dressed as Radha and Krishna participate, and the dramatic portion.

> The Swami sings the devotional hymn: "Radhey-Radhey-Govind, Govind-Radhey." The Samajis and the audience join in. Some devotee, a bearded sadhu or a close-shaven priest, comes into the area zealously clanging large metal tongs studded with brass bells and chanting the words. The audience claps in time with his chant, losing itself in the *dhun* (the melody). As the tempo rises, he grows more and more vigorous. He is possessed and makes the audience possessed. At a peak of excitement all together stand up and rock and sway their arms overhead, clapping rhythmically and shouting the melody in quick gasps. This binds the devotee to the Lord Krishna. (Gargi, 124)

The medieval *ras* would appear to derive from an earlier form such as the three-day *Kaniyar Kali* of the Bhagavati cult, in which dancers circle a large lighted lamp to vocal and instrumental music in a representation of the dance of Kali (Pisharoti, 169). This is also followed by dramatic enactment, but of a comic and satirical kind.

Probably the oldest circular trance dance, or that which most approximates the Churning of the Ocean, is found in the *Lai Haraoba* festival of Manipur. Led by the shamanistic *maibi* and *maiba* mediums, it dates from prehistoric Shaivaism and Tantric cults. "Lai" is said to be a corruption of "*linga*" (Singh, 30), and the pole used in the churning in one version of the myth is said to be Shiva's *linga*, also representing the axis of the world (Gonda, 128).

The drama in the medieval *raslila* is characteristic of several theatre forms developed in this period, based on the use of tableaux for devotional purposes.

> At the climax of the chanting the curtain is removed and a tableau is revealed, a beautiful pictorial vision of Radha and

Krishna. The leader shouts an elongated slogan, "*Radhaiaiai . . . ,*" and the audience answers, ". . . *Shyam!*" This transforms the acting arena into a temple where Krishna and Radha, represented by two innocent boys, are the object of worship. Incense is burnt, and gifts and money are offered. (Gargi, 125)

Each day a different episode from Krishna's life is performed in the *lila* portion of the dance drama, and these are punctuated throughout by tableaux, creating a particular kind of dramatic unity suitable to the devotional and ecstatic characteristics of the *bhakti* movement. In a similar manner, the *Ramlila*, which lasts thirty days and is performed in different locations, is structured upon tableaux, some of which can last for an hour, based on scenes from the *Ramayana*. It is possible to consider medieval painting an influence upon this drama, and perhaps it was so, but Radha and Krishna seated for adoration in the *raslila* are most clearly living statues, just as actual statues might be worshiped in this way, and such practices must account for its origins. The archaic form of living statue is represented by the trance mediums of Bhagavati, who sit giving oracles in their elaborate costumes.

One particular image of the *raslila* may be traced directly from this source. It is that of the performers playing Radha and Krishna seated on a swing for adoration in the festival of *jhulan yatra* (Devi, 179). In West India, "followers dress the image of the god [Krishna] in clothes, adorn it with ornaments, rock it on a decorated swing, and offer it food" (Gargi, 117). The shaman of South India has a "swing cot . . . on which is placed a figurine made of brass or bronze in the shape of a human being, tiger, boar or bison," which he worships every day (Ranganath, 32). The deity residing in such an image is fed, and the shaman himself swings on "three semicircular blades [attached] to three pairs of chains from the roof beams" (Harper, 272). We have noted that demons entering the Ceylonese *gam meduva* exorcism rock for a while on a swing. The metaphysical meaning would appear to be a "suspension" of being which is "not of this earth," and the relation of trance to statue in shamanism has been carried from shamanism into representation in the *raslila*.

Another aspect of the medieval drama that relates it to earlier modes of performance is represented by the use of huge paper effigies of the demons Ravana and Kumbhakarna in the *Ramlila*. They are similar in design to the huge figures in the *kolam* or to the gigantic effigies of planetary gods and demons used in Ceylonese *bali* exorcism rituals. The *bali* figures are destroyed for ritualistic reasons after the curing cere-

8. Two demons in the *sanniyakuma* rock slowly on a swing.

mony, while the *Ramlila* demons are destroyed by fire for reasons of spectacle. Still, they would seem to derive from typical forms of the demon play, such as that performed in Malaya to honor Subramanya, Shiva's son.

> On this day the epic war with Sooran, called *Sooran Por*, is enacted in the temple as a pantomime. The statues of Subramanya as war leader and of Sooran with his six successive heads are carried into the compound on a ramp. The felling of each head by the God is dramatized. As the final head falls, devotees shout *"Vel, Vel"* and the deity is carried victoriously back into the temple. On the seventh day the worshippers break fast.   (Arasaratnam, 42)

Sanskrit drama is preeminently identified with the *nataka*, its most highly developed and sophisticated type of play. Of the ten *rupakas*, or "regular" plays conforming with the codes of performance outlined by Bharata, the third and fifth in importance show the adaptation of the demon play. The *samavakara*, which "is borrowed from the legends of gods and demons," was to have "at least twelve known and exalted heroes, gods or men, each of whom pursues a special aim" (Konow, 45). The *dima* was to have sixteen leading characters "who are all impetuous ... gods, gandharvas, yaksas, raksasas, serpent-demons (nagas), bhutas, pretas, pisacas, etc.," most of these being types of demon. "Hurricanes, meteors, the solar and the lunar eclipses, fight, struggle and sorcery make their appearances here" (Konow, 47).

The *Natyashastra* (IV,9–11) says that a *dima* entitled *Tripuradaha* (*The Burning of Tripura, the Triple City*) was presented following the Churning of the Ocean, and it was thus the third play ever performed. It was acted for Shiva in the Himalayan region, so that the meaning here might be in regard to religious or theatrical influence from that area. More probably, the reference to the mountains is metaphysical. The basic meaning in regard to the origins of drama must relate to the nature of the Triple City, which was constructed by Maya, architect of the demons or antigods and creator of the science of magic. This city was destroyed by Shiva (Danielou, 315). Since drama "descended from the heavens" after this performance, Bharata's identification of Tripura with it seems to have been his means of representing a demon play still associated with the "architecture" of delusion or hallucination as a factor in the perception of performance.

The "descent of drama from the heavens" was caused by another type of *rupaka* called the *prahasana*, a farce. Actors "practiced in course of time an art tiring the entire people with Prahasanas connected with laughter ... a play which caricatured the sages and which was unacceptable and full of wicked acts, and which encouraged rural manners and was cruel and inauspicious" (XXXVI,33–35; Ghosh, II, 233). We have noted that satire can develop from, and be performed with, the demon play, as in Tibet or Korea. Sanskrit drama performed three types of *prahasana*: the pure (*suddha*), in which "the sectarians, the brahmins and all kinds of low-standing persons appear—each speaking his own distinctive tongue and remaining devoted to his own profession"; the mixed (*samkirna*), in which "hetaeras, slaves, eunuchs, epicureans (*vita*) and rogues (*dhūrta*) appear"; and the disfigured (*vikrta*), in which "eunuchs, chamberlains, etc. in costume and speech, appear as lovers" (Konow, 48–49). The reform of this low state of drama was accomplished when the king offered to place performance under his protection and patronage. The *devadasis* then brought to the *nataka* the *srngara* (erotic) *rasa* (sentiment) which, with the heroic *rasa*, characterizes this type of play, but their contribution would seem to relate more to their role as courtesans as an aspect of narrative than to dance technique used in drama. The main influences which shaped the *nataka* under court patronage were poetic and literary, but it is still possible to perceive underlying elements of dramatic structure which account for its origins.

The end of an act of a *nataka* is marked by the exit of all characters from the stage, suggesting that it is based on the compartmentalized series of scenes characteristic of the demon play. Continuity between scenes or acts is maintained by five kinds of interlude used as means of explaining the action, most often in Prakrit rather than in Sanskrit. The characters of the interludes are lower-class persons who are often represented as being members of the theatrical company itself. In this we see a development of the role of the *sutradhara*, the "holder of the thread" of the narrative. The *sutradhara*, as director or stage manager, is himself frequently represented in the interludes. In the introduction, the *sutradhara* characteristically appears in conversation with other persons—his wife, his assistant, or the *vidusaka*, a clown figure.

The *vidusaka* also relates to the internal construction of scenes, for he appears there as a companion of the hero. The striking makeup of the *vidusaka*, with spots and lines and darkened eye and mustache areas, as well as the crown-like hat, clearly show him to be derived from a comic demon evolved from ritual exorcism. "He is a humpbacked dwarf with projected teeth and distorted face; he is bald-headed and yellow-eyed; he covers himself with tatters and skins and anoints himself with ashes, etc." (Konow, 23). It appears that he might sometimes wear a wig and beard (Bhat, 48). Maru Sanniya, the most feared demon in the *sanni-yakuma*, does not wear a mask as do the other demons, but his face is blackened, he has false teeth stuck in his mouth, and he wears a shaggy black wig and beard (Sarathchandra, 40), makeup which is very like that of the *vidusaka*.

The *vidusaka* is one of the members of a small court which the hero has around him and by means of which the action can be carried forward in dialogue based on the confidant relationship. The *vita*, an epicurean and raconteur, lends color to this group and would appear to derive from the *bhana* type of *rupaka*, which is a one-act monologue in which the *vita* "partly describes his own experiences and partly those of others" and "pretends as if he sees and hears others acting and speaking" (Konow, 49). The technique of the *bhana* seems to be the basis of the *vithi* type of *rupaka*, a one-act play performed by two actors, in which "there appear many conversations with imaginary persons" (Konow, 50). The probability that this monologue technique, a characteristic of Indian drama, developed from the presentation of a trance medium as oracle, giving social comment and observations, has been suggested above. The *nataka* would then have developed, just as the *Natyashastra* tells us, from trance exorcism that had become comedy, a form to which sophisticated literary tastes were then applied in the creation of legendary, heroic romances.

Chapter III

CHINA:
MEDIUMS, MUSICIANS,
AND ACROBATS

The history of Chinese theatre presents us with a bewildering succession of modes in which one form of regional theatre, usually named for its place of origin, replaces another form in popular favor and extends its influence into other regions of the country. Yet the basic characteristics of the Peking-style drama, the national or classic theatre that developed in the early years of the nineteenth century, go back in an unbroken continuum for at least one thousand years prior to that time. It appears that the more than three hundred different regional forms found today vary only in use of local dialects and musical styles.

It is generally known that Chinese drama "traces its origins back to the song and dance which accompanied festivals and religious or public ceremonies of ancient times" (Scott, 28). A. E. Zucker cites the Chinese shamanism of 2000 B. C. in this regard and suggests a continuing influence. "It can be seen readily that the more or less spontaneous and popular mimicry of the *wu* (mediums) would naturally enough be suppressed at this time [1122 B. C.]; but in later dynasties we find again many references to the beauty, the splendid costumes, the singing and dancing, and in general the charm of these actors in popular religious ceremonies" (Zucker, 7–8). It seems that "it has been widely thought that the beginnings of theatrical representation were connected with shamanistic religious celebrations..." (Mackerras [G], 58). These origins can be reconstructed in some detail.

9. Chinese medium with makeup like that of the classic theatre standing with a spirit flag used in exorcism before an altar which seems to have prefigured the all-purpose table used on stage.

10. The deity who guards holy places, as represented in a Nepalese demon play.

11. A general on the classic Chinese stage wearing flags on his back, as does the deity in the Nepalese exorcism. The inner sleeves that hide the emperor's hands were once a mediumistic manner of representing ghosts.

12. Scene from a Na-khi ceremony, southwest China, showing a theatrical arrangement of performers. The trees are for the gods to repose on when they descend.

13. Priest in the Na-khi ceremony performing the part of the spirit of victory, wearing armor, helmet with pheasant feathers and with face painted to frighten the enemy.

First, shamanism (or spirit mediumship) is the origin of the "painted face" role which is characteristic of Chinese drama. Chang says that the painted face of any Buddha, god, ghost, or demon in the plays was "derived from the transformation of the spiritual operas which were concerned with driving away a plague or exorcizing a ghost" (Chang, 46). More significant, however, is that this is the derivation of face painting itself as a principle. Face painting is used to represent forceful as well as evil characters and those lacking in social standing in the *ching* or "painted face" category of role, and a different stylization of painted face is used for the clowns and foolish characters in the *chou* category. It appears that there were only two roles in the theatre of the Tang dynasty (A.D. 618–906), the hero and the villain, the latter a painted-face role (Chou, 76). This suggests an origin in a basic conflict between good and evil, with face painting identified with the demonic. The *chou* clown category seems to appear first in a minor role in the Yuan dynasty (1277–1368), and it apparently again represents comedy developed from the demonic.

The *ching* painted-face roles appear in both major categories of drama, the civic and the military plays, and their use for magistrates and other officials seems related also in character type and costume to the representation of generals as *ching* in the military plays, and seems to have derived from this source. Here we find an association of face painting with costume which relates the representation of *ching* generals directly to the practices of spirit mediumship. It has been thought that the four flags supported from the back of a *ching* general on the stage derive from flags once worn in this way by generals on the battlefield and passed to subordinates "to prove the authenticity of an order" (Zung, 22), or waved "to direct the movements of troops" (Arlington, 86). However, the flags do not derive from actual war, but rather from the practices of metaphysical war against the spirits of evil. The Tibetan shaman has "on his back vari-colored paper flags which are stuck in his girdle," and over magnificent brocade garments and apron he wears on his chest a mirror of gilt silver (Rock, 798, 811). The costume is similar to the embroidered satin gown known as "armor" on the Chinese stage, and the mirror to the "heart-protecting glass" which is worn with it (Zung, 21). In Chinese mediumship, the flags fan upward from the back of the sedan chair in which the medium is carried in exorcistic processions (Elliott, 64ff.). The flags represent the five major divisions of the Celestial Army—central, north, south, east, and west—commanded by thirty-six generals of the heavenly force's struggle against evil. The medium is often possessed by the spirit of one of these generals, and thus enacts his presence and person upon the stage of the seance.

In the great exorcistic processions of the Han dynasty (206 B.C.–A.D.220), "men having their faces painted black, red, green, or otherwise, with dishevelled hair, whips, swords, or bells, on horseback or afoot, bear live snakes around their necks," representing and manifesting in trance incarnations the generals of the Celestial Army (de Groot, 985). This use of solid colors at such an early date would lend some credence to a general theory that stage makeup has become more complex as it evolved. The painted faces of the Ming period (1368–1644) and of the Ch'ing dynasty (1644–1911) leave the chin bare and emphasize basic solid colors with patterned bands sweeping upward diagonally from the eyes (Chiu-yao, 82ff.; Zung, 39). The present-day medium paints his face to represent General Chao; the black-faced commander of the Celestial Army; Monkey, represented by curvilinear designs; and other characters that possess him in trance. The temples have theatres, and theatrical performances to please the *shen* are given at the same time as seances. Makeup styles must represent a continued symbiotic relationship between stage and mediumship. Some Peking designs still reproduce the four-eyed *fang-siang*, which dates from the Han, and differing complexity is probably due more to regional preference than to an evolution of form. The Bon shaman of China and Tibet can wear a complex curvilinear pattern, like that often found in Peking drama, as well as more simplified patterns (see Rock [N], xviii, xix). Theatrical face painting clearly derives from mediumship and most probably from the ancient Bon shamanism which extended from Siberia to the southwestern part of China.

The basic staging and conventions of the Chinese theatre appear to derive directly from mediumship. The stage is bare except for a table and chairs, which are used in a number of ways to represent various scenic pieces, such as a throne or a mountain. The table is similar in form to the offerings table, sometimes called an altar, which is an essential part of all mediumistic ceremonies, and it clearly derives from it. The wall of the temple behind the offerings table is often like that of the theatre, with a doorway to right and to left. In the theatre, these doorways are called "spirit doors," and entrances are almost invariably made from the one on the left, which is called the "upper" doorway, and exits by means of the one on the right, called the "lower" doorway. The terminology would seem to derive from the fact that the spirit which possesses a medium is thought to descend and thus always to enter or appear from above.

The medium sometimes dresses "back stage" in the costume of the role he will play, but it is usual practice that the costume be completed "on stage," after the medium has been possessed by a particular spirit, and at this time a decorated apron symbolizing the spirit is placed on him by assistants. In this we may see the origin of the convention in which the actors sometimes turn toward the back wall and change their garments in view of the audience, aided by a group of assistants who have no actual roles in the drama being performed.

When the spirit leaves the medium at the end of a performance, he characteristically "gives a great leap into the air and falls back into the arms of assistants" (Elliott, 101). In the Chinese theatre, a character who is shocked or horrified will fall to the floor completely rigid or will suddenly, without preparation, perform a backward somersault with lightning speed (Kalvodová [B], 513). Such stylization of action was most probably suggested by the behavior of the medium. In the technique of the percussive music which accompanies and drives on the actions of the medium, so that "while the gong resounds more loudly and quickly . . . he starts forward at a gallop or trot" (de Groot, 1280), the origins of similar uses of music on the stage are apparent.

A difference in musical mode seems to be the most important factor that distinguishes the various types of Chinese drama. It is noted that in general there is a northern style, which is vivid, bold, and loud, and a southern style, which is softer and more melodious. Thus, the *I-yang ch'iang*, which developed in Kiangsi province in the early sixteenth century, was said to be "really hard on the ears of a refined person," since "its cymbals are very noisy and its sung sections disorderly and clamorous" (Mackerras, 4–5). On the other hand, the *K'un-ch'u*, which originated about the same time in Kiangsu province, presented music dominated by flutes and lutes and was said to be "very melancholy," moving people to tears, and "soft and melodious" (Mackerras, 7). The regional stylistic contrast in music seems to relate to the two types of play. The orchestra in Chinese theatre is divided in accord with the civil and military categories of drama, with string and most wind instruments classed as civil, and percussion instruments, such as drums, gongs, and cymbals, being classed as military (Arlington, 25). The two categories of play seem to be represented by contrasting modes of stylized action, with the military plays full of spectacular, bravura athleticism, while the nonmilitary "dotes on the scrupulously controlled falsetto voice and the mincing step" (Crump, 421). The contrast clearly suggests different origins for each of the two modes. A reasonable hypothesis in this regard would be that the military derived from what de Groot calls the "savage music" of drums, gongs, and cymbals used in exorcistic processions and ceremonies, while the melodic modes derived from elegant and lyric dances by means of which the shamanesses "brought down" the deities who possessed them. In this sense, which may only be metaphorical, they are masculine and feminine modes. The male spirit medium's seance is accompanied by the sound of drums and gongs played by some half a dozen youths, the noise of which "can be tremendous" and "is particularly obnoxious to evil spirits and conducive to the descent of the *shen" (Elliott, 52).* The **"masculine,"** exorcistic noise music of the military mode has brought with it a wide range of spectacular theatricality and forceful stylization, while the "feminine" was responsible for introducing beautiful lyric qualities and graceful stylization importantly associated with song, poetry, and narrative literature. However, there were companies composed entirely of women, and women perform the spectacular acrobatics associated with military plays, just as men perform in the more delicate style, so that the contrast based on sex is meant essentially as a hypothesis of probable origins.

Arlington describes the acrobatic battles and musical accompaniment of Peking-style military plays as follows:

All actors must be absolutely correct in every one of their movements, and in time with the music. The conscious agility, *fougé*, and precision which fill the performer become contagious and delight the spectators as well. What frequently attracts the attention is a confusion of swirling colour, which suddenly clears when an actor, holding a mighty weapon, comes to a full stop at the footlights. Off the stage struts this fearfully painted warrior, followed by companies of soldiers who once more continue the din and confusion of a fierce battle. During the performance, the spectator's ears are violently assaulted by the sound of drums, gong, fiddles, castanets, and other diabolical instruments of torture. He is so bewildered by scenes of fighting, tumbling, whirling on one leg, rushing to and fro, yelling and screeching, that, to use one of our own expressions, he imagines that "Bedlam has broken loose!"   (Arlington, 4)

The basic source of such spectacular battle scenes, in which banners on poles are swept over and under tumblers as they somersault through the air, or in which amazing, gymnastic, precisely choreographed encounters with swords occur, is to be found in the use of banners and swords in exorcistic spectacles. In one such exorcism, for example, the *ki tong* spirit medium climbs a ladder of swords barefoot, aided by the *sai kong* exorcist and other members of the group who function in specialized roles.

> When this moment has come, the *ki tông*, who has professedly observed the vigil of seven or ten days, prepares to climb the ladder with dishevelled hair, wearing his embroidered stomacher, his sword in hand. The chief among the officiating *sai kong* clears the rungs before-hand from spectres by spattering or spurting water which is mixed with ashes of exorcising charms, and by throwing up rice and salt, at the same time ringing his hand-bell, blowing his horn, and uttering spells. An ear-splitting noise of gongs and drums resounds, and the *lô iên sê*, shaking their rings, mutter spells which bring down the Celestial Army and its generals. As they call the northern army, a *hoat tiúng* takes position at the north side of the ladder, waving a black banner, and pacing out a magic figure on the ground; he, or another, then furiously cleaves the air with perpendicular strokes. And in the same wise the four other cardinal points are operated on by four *hoat tiúng*, each with a banner of the colour which represents his cardinal point; thus, indeed, all demons are sabred away, and the five celestial army-divisions, assembled by those banners, bravely perform their salutary work of destruction of spectres.   (de Groot, 1291)

Sword dances are also still practiced in connection with mediumship, as by a group of youths in trance, wearing special costumes and dancing before the offering table which has been set up outside the temple (Elliott, 125). In the theatre, such dances merged at a very early period with the various types of pseudo-shamanistic popular entertainments.

> [Performances] soon came to include such feats of strength and skill as tumbling, somersaulting, ropewalking, poleclimbing, tripod-lifting, swordswallowing, firespitting, and many others, to form the so-called Hundred Entertainments. Sometimes the players disguised themselves as leopards and bears, tigers and dragons, fairies, and nymphs, and sang amidst floating clouds and drifting snowflakes.
> (Wu-chi, 159)

Such acts were the basis of the variety shows called *tsa-hsi*, "mixed plays," which were performed in the Ch'in to Han dynasties (255–207 B.C.) (Arlington, 8). We can see the continuation of this tradition in another description of the Peking-style military plays by a certain Hsü K'o.

[Performers] must be able to leap aloft and drop like a falling sparrow, travel upside down and spin in dance like a whirlwind . . . they ascend or descend ropes and poles like monkeys, and toss their bodies about like autumn leaves. Each is able to bear on his chest a pyramid of five men, and also can vault atop a structure twenty to thirty feet high. Such acrobatic skill is not easily come by, however, so what is actually required for the military stage is the ability to make fists and swords fly . . . so that he darts convincingly hither and thither in mock battle, and in the instant when he is hardest pressed there is a glitter of swords, and his body flashes like an arrow.   (Crump, 421)

The magic acts of pseudo-shamanism have also held a place in these spectacles, as in the effects of the Szechwan stage in which an actor's face is ":magically" transformed in color and aspect by secretly blowing into a pile of powdered pigment or by pulling off a sequence of silk masks with the aid of strings (Kalvodová [B], 515–16).

The second mode of music and dramatic action, the lyric and graceful, which is associated primarily but not exclusively with the "civil" plays and with the drama of southern China, is first found in *The Songs of the South*, which probably date from the fourth century B.C. but may be much earlier. There "male and female shamans—it is not always clear which—having first purified and perfumed themselves and dressed up in gorgeous costumes, sing and dance to the accompaniment of music, drawing the gods down from heaven in a sort of divine courtship" (Hawkes, 35). Some of the poems are clearly meant for performance; others describe the ceremonies.

The singing begins softly to a slow, solemn measure;
Then, as pipes and zithers join in, the singing grows shriller.
Now the priestesses come, splendid in their gorgeous apparel,
And all the hall is filled with a penetrating fragrance.
The five sounds mingle in a rich harmony;
And the god is merry and takes his pleasure.
                                                              (Hawkes, 36)

The word *wu* can mean "shaman" or "to dance," and one of the calligraphic characters for "shaman" seems to represent "a man with long sleeves gracefully dancing" (L. Hopkins, 9). A Fancy Sleeve Dance was performed in the Han dynasty (206 B.C.–A.D. 220) (Chang, 2). In general, the aesthetic of this shamanistic dance mode must have been similar to that of the Japanese *miko* shamaness. The aesthetic, as such, is beautifully expressed in the noh play dance of Hyakuman, which was based on the dance of the *miko*.

My fluttering sleeves tell of my hope
That I shall meet my child.
My fluttering sleeves tell of my hope
That parent and child shall meet.
Watch, then, the dance of Hyakuman.
My sleeves dance a hundred times
And then ten thousand,
As I pray to know
Where my child has gone.

(O'Neill, 150)

This suggests what I take to be the shamanistic origin of the extensive "vocabulary" of sleeve positions and sleeve uses which characterize performance in the Chinese drama. The normally full sleeves of the brocaded robes are extended by white cuffs of sheer silk about eighteen inches in length which can be kept tucked within the sleeve or used in the more than fifty different kinds of sleeve movements which comprise a kind of gesture system indicating stylized basic attitudes. The added appendage of the white cuffs appears to have originated in the representation of ghosts, since a standing position with the arms at the sides so that the cuffs hang down over the hands can only be taken by an actor playing a ghost.

The origin of Chinese theatre is represented by the mythological figure of Lan Ts'ai-ho, one of the Eight Immortals of Taoism and "the patron saint of itinerant actors" (van Gulik, 124). The strolling singer or mountebank of the Immortals, Lan, is either a young man or a girl shown playing a flute, cymbals, or a pair of clappers. The facts that Lan was often said to have been an hermaphrodite and was taken for a lunatic seem to reflect shamanistic sex change and hysteria. All of the Eight Immortals appear to represent the pseudo-shamanism of "itinerant Taoist priests who earned their living by banning devils, selling charms and pills and engaging in tricks of various kinds and the art of juggling in order to convince the multitude of their supernatural powers" (van Gulik, 118). Ts'ao Kuo Chiu is also said to be the patron saint of theatrical performance, or of musicians when he carries a pair of clappers, but there is little relevant material about him, unless the beating of an innocent woman with "iron-spiked whips," an incident that leads to his apotheosis, is an allegorical reference to the use of prick balls in mediumistic self-punishment, as it well might be. Han Hsiang Tzu, the patron saint of fortunetellers, represented with a bamboo drum and pair of clappers, could make marvelous flowering plants grow suddenly from a little earth in a flower pot, the famous "mango trick" which Chinese pseudo-shamanism seems to have derived from India. In a similar manner, Lu Tung-pin, patron of devil banners, armed with a sword to suppress demons, could turn water into wine, while Chang Kuo, depicted with a bamboo drum and clappers, entertained the emperor with magical performances. In this differentiation of shamanism into itinerant popular entertainments, ballad singing was probably most important in the development of drama.

It is generally believed that Chinese theatre developed during the Sung and Yuan dynasties (A.D. 969–1368) from the songs which wandering musicians performed on street corners and in marketplaces and from a linking of their popular folk songs into a pattern of minimal dramatic action. Sung-dynasty (A.D. 969–1277) playwrights often incorporated the Big Song, which had been introduced in the Tang (618–907), "an elaborate form of poetry containing a group or sequence of ten or more songs preceded by a prologue and ending with an epilogue" (Wu-chi, 165). Another mode, practiced about the same time, was *ku-tzu-tz'u*, the Drum Song, or "drum singing." "The best known example of the genre consists of a reading of a famous tale interspersed with song-poems (all to the same tune) at appropriate places. We can be sure that music certainly, and dance probably, were part of the performance" (Crump [Y], 477). The Drum Song of the itinerant performers is thought to have devleoped into the Medley which "has a unique structure of alternate recitative and sung parts, the latter constituting the main bulk of the poem, being chanted to the accompaniment of stringed instruments" (Wu-chi, 172). We have noted the account of the two shamanesses who "were dressed very gaudily, and chanted and danced excellently," opening with bells and drums and alternating this with the music of stringed instruments and bamboo pipes (de Groot, 1213).

When enacted by a number of performers, the ballad songs seem to have become the *nan-hsi*, the southern drama of the Sung, which was partly based on local folk songs and had seven types of actor, including the *ching* painted face and the *chou* clown, who had a "face daubed with black powder and was very ugly" (Mackerras, 2). In the north during this same period the ballad forms became the *tsa-chu* (Variety Play), four acts of linked tunes in which it is thought only the leading performer sang, although he or she might play different characters in each of the acts. It appears that Yuan dramas "if reduced to their skeletons, consist of nothing but dramatically organized sets of lyric poems or songs" (Crump [Y], 477), although it has also been observed in regard to the *tsa-chu* that "prose dialogue generally occupies two-thirds of a play" (Waley [S], 89).

The subject matter of the plays appears to have developed from that of the folk songs. Most plays of the Yuan period (A.D. 1277–1368) can be grouped in the following categories: (1) love and intrigue; (2) religious and supernatural; (3) historical and pseudo-historical; (4) domestic and social; (5) murder and lawsuit; (6) bandit-hero (Wu-chi, 171). The "military" mode, using shorter song sets, cuts across these categories.

The only extant text which seems to show the pre-Yuan type of variety play is a comic scenario in which four characters plan to "call down" the Eight Immortals, rather like a parody of mediumship (Crump, 427–28). In a poem written in the early thirteenth century (Sung), a rustic on his first visit to an urban playhouse is surprised that the orchestra composed of women is not practicing the usual mediumship.

> Some females there were sitting facing the stage—
> Not calling the spirits down like they do in our country gambols,
> But ceaselessly banging the drums and clashing of cymbals.
>
> (Hawkes [R], 75)

As late as the eighteenth century, it was explained of a staging of the *Mu-lien* play that "it was performed at the end of the year; various spirits and werewolves would come out to replace the exorcisms of ancient times" (Mackerras, 255).

Until quite recent times, village folk plays that contributed to the various styles of regional drama were still performed. In them, we can see a reflection of the process which formed the more ancient drama and which continued to transform the "mainstream" styles, largely by contributing different musical modes. The *teng-hsi* folk play of the mountainous region of northern Szechwan was performed by village shamans who wore carved and painted masks in their exorcism ceremonies but painted their faces for performance of the plays. At first, the cast was comprised of three members, one of whom played women's roles, and action was accompanied by two musicians who played in turn upon a drum, a gong, and a type of violin. Dialogue predominated, with themes being based on folklore and legend, and the music was a variant of a folk song which provided a single motif for each play. This use of a single motif is like that which characterized each act of the *tsa-chu* variety play, and all of the early forms appear to have been equally simple in their staging at their inception. About ten of the fifty *teng-hsi* plays found their way to the professional stage of the cities at the beginning of this century, exemplifying the process which has produced the changing modes within Chinese theatre (Kalvodová, 515–16). In discussing the importance of this type of play, Kalvodová also appears to have accepted a common Marxist version of the Victorian vegetation theory, suitable because it represents an ethos of folk labor, which relates dramatic origins to Rice Planting Plays "built up round motions familiar to the country people in their daily life, like the motions of different jobs in the fields" (Kalvodová, 505). I doubt that it can be shown that the imitative actions of simple work dances ever led to dramas performed on other occasions or that there is any relation to the shamanistic folk plays.

It has been observed that the *tsa-chu* variety play of the Yuan (A.D. 1277–1368) "seems to have become familiar to virtually every part of China" during this period (Mackerras, 3). That this was the case cannot be attributed only to the itinerant singers and performers associated with the pseudo-shamanistic Hundred Entertainments, so that a form was borrowed from them outright, but to the fact that the plays could readily be adopted by an existing mode of performance, the shamanistic ceremonies of spirit possession and exorcism which had existed in all regions of China from ancient times. This similarity between ritual and theatrical modes then continued to influence regional styles and the "mainstream" of performance usually identified with modes performed in Peking.

Chapter IV

JAPAN: NOH DRAMA; THE SUN IN A CAVE

The noh is a highly stylized, extremely serious, chanted dance-drama, yet it has been thought that it originated in vulgar farces and buffoonery. It is "generally accepted as fact" that noh drama originated in a type of comic performance called *sarugaku* (Araki, 39). "The farcical representations in the sarugaku are believed to have provided the two basic elements of drama—dialogue and mimicry—and the nō is believed to have come into existence when music and dance were added to this" (Araki, 59). Yet this theory has seemed unsatisfactory. "The suddenness and completeness of the transformation from saragaku to nō is a mystifying phenomenon indeed" (Araki, 59). The problem is complicated by the fact that there were several major types of noh— *saragaku* noh, *dengaku* noh, *ennen* noh, and *Shugen* noh—as well as minor local variants. "The connections between these forms of Ennen Nō and Sarugaku and Dengaku Nō, especially the question of which arose first, is still uncertain" (O'Neill, 99). It is thought that "various dramatic dances which had attained a degree of acknowledged grace" were added to the vulgar farces in each type of performance until they became "highly developed, dignified, and artistic forms" (Lombard, 74). But for some it has been difficult to believe that noh drama owed anything to crude farces, and for formal and aesthetic reasons an origin in ritual dances has been presented as an alternative theory. Thus, William Ridgeway argued that there were "two distinct lines of dramatic evolution in Japan."

... the purity and freedom from all grossness ... point to [the noh
dramas] not having been evolved from the comic *dengaku* or
sarugaku ... but rather all through, from the primitive *kagura* to
their full development, to have been solemn, moral, and free from
grossness.   (Ridgeway, 329–31)

The concept of an origin from the ritualistic *kagura* would find some
support in Japanese tradition, but it would appear that this theory, too,
is incorrect.

The idea that noh originated in *kagura* may be traced to the same
source that has provided the only basis for the concept of an origin
from primitive comedy. Both theories depend upon readings of, and
attributions to, an episode in classical Shinto mythology as represented
in the *Kojiki* (*Records of Ancient Matters*, A.D. 682–712). It tells how
the goddess Uzume danced to lure the sun goddess, Amaterasu, from
the cave in which she had hidden. Independent traditional attributions
of the origins of both noh and *kagura* to this dance have led to the
belief that noh derived from *kagura*. Arnott refers to "the tradition
deriving the *Noh* from the *Kagura* stage and the latter from the up-
turned tub on which Ame-no-uzume-no-miko danced; the characteristic
stamping of the *Noh* dance is said to originate from the pounding of the
feet that lured the goddess out" (Arnott, 63–64). Zeami, the first
theoretician of noh, recounted how the goddess Uzume "came forward
and danced and sang, divinely inspired, bearing a branch of the *sakaki*
tree ... making sacred bonfires, and stamping—thump, thump—with
her feet." He did not mention *kagura* specifically but observed that
"the divine music and dance at that time is said to be the very
beginning of Sarugaku" (Zeami, 54).

Various ritual preparations in the *Kojiki*, such as divining by burning
deer bones, are shamanistic, and the spirit possession and consequent
dance of the "divinely inspired" Uzume is "a vivid shamanistic performance" (Fairchild, 47–48). Ryūzō Torii reportedly "asserts that shamanism was the native religion of the Japanese, that the sun-goddess and
the deities surrounding her ... were shamans, and that the whole
setting for the concealment myth is shamanistic" (Philippi, 84). A most
important factor in luring Amaterasu from the cave is an uprooted
evergreen tree which is decorated with a large mirror, strings of beads,
and cloth offerings. The ritualized *sakaki* tree is again the shamanistic
tree as a kind of "lightning rod" for descent of the spirit in possession.
A similar principle is involved in the branch said to have been carried by

Uzume and in the "various objects" held by another goddess as "solemn offerings" for the ritual, if it is correct that "these were probably not offerings in the strict sense, but implements held in the hands of the shaman in order to induce possession by the spirit of the deity" (Philippi, 83). The objects worshiped in *kagura* dances are suggested.

Shamanic trance possession, like the noh and *kagura*, is generally not vulgar or comic. Yet it is said that when Uzume "became divinely possessed, [she] exposed her breasts, and pushed her skirt-band down to her genitals" (Philippi, 84), or that she engaged in "pulling out the nipples of her breasts, [and] pushing down her skirt-string *usque ad privatas partes*" (Chamberlain, 69), thus causing the laughter of the assembled gods. This has led to the assumptions that "originally primitive kagura must have been chiefly a comic dance" (Perkins and Fujii, 62), or that *mikagura* (court *kagura*) originally "contained some funny actions" which have "since been lost" (Inoura, 20), or that "comic dances (saru-mahi or monkey-dances) . . . were the origin of the Kagura and Nō performances" (Aston, 79). But the apparent lewdness is more probably an aspect of the nature and style of the *Kojiki* than a record of the characteristics of an actual dance or type of trance possession. William Griffis observed that "the dominant note throughout the *Kojiki* is abundant filthiness" (Griffis, 66), and its translator commented upon its "shocking obscenity of word and act" and its "naive filthiness" (Chamberlain, xlvii). Scatological and erotic imagery, such as defecation in Amaterasu's kitchen or an onanistic act done in fear with a shuttle, is used as a conceptual means of representing symbolic acts and relationships. In this context, the nature of Uzume's dance seems to refer to (1) the subjective nature of shamanic trance, a kind of "spiritual nakedness"; (2) the basic hysteria often associated with shamanic possession; and (3) the "mystical marriage" of the shamaness and the god, a type of trance experience which appears to have contributed to a close identification of shamanism and prostitution in Japan.

The goddess Amaterasu also represents the concept of shamanic experience as such. A mirror is an important ritual instrument in shamanism, and the mirror attached to the sakaki tree in the myth plays the decisive role in Amaterasu's emergence from the cave. She leaves her sanctuary when she becomes entranced with her own image in the mirror, believing that an unknown, more illustrious deity is present. The function of the mirror is undoubtedly meant as an illustration of that of the shamans throughout Asia who use it as a means of concentrating to the point of self-hypnosis and thus achieve the trance state (Eliade, 153–54). The sun-within-the-cave image is not "a naive explanation of a solar eclipse" (Sakanishi, 3) but a body-consciousness metaphor in which Amaterasu represents the god who emerged, and emanated as voice, from within the shaman. The "light" she sheds on the world is that of the benefits which shamanism provided for society. Her withdrawal into the "cave" symbolizes a withdrawal of shamanic god consciousness from the world *within* the world, within the human body, a breaking of the shamanistic link between man and divinity which is then reestablished by Uzume's dance.

Uzume and Amaterasu together thus form a composite double image of shamanic experience, as if the latter were the deity made manifest in the spirit possession and entranced dance of the former. In this relationship, however, it is the lesser goddess Uzume who represents mortals (Fairchild, 30). It would seem that the laughter of the assembled gods at Uzume's dance is a structural technique, a conceptual means of emphasizing the subservient role of mortals in this relationship and the fact that they do not have actual control over the gods who possess them; hence the laughter of the assembled deities.

I do not believe, therefore, that either the lewd or the comic aspects of Uzume's dance can be considered apart from the symbolic context of the myth in which they appear nor that they should or can be understood as representing characteristics of an actual dance or type of dance. The traditional attribution of the origin of both noh and *kagura* to this dance would be secondary to, and would depend upon, its primary shamanistic meaning and would indicate only that the shamanistic origins of these forms were known and recognized. The attribution of both forms to a shamanic dance should not be taken, as it has been, to imply that the noh developed from *kagura* dances. In fact, "all performing artists in Japan claim descent from the heavenly dancer Uzume" (Immoos, 404), and no precedence of forms, other than from trance possession, can be recognized.

The origin of the *matsuri* festivals is also attributed to the dance of Uzume. In one such festival, the shamanistic origins of noh drama are still commemorated. The great Yogo Pine at Nara is said to have "provided a passage for the descent of Nō from the world of the gods to the world of men," and there this origin is reenacted annually. A "spirit" descends through the "vertical axis" of the tree to a dancer beneath, inducing trance and causing him to move "at the will of a god as his creature, a medium possessed of the divine spirit" (Keene, 35). The single pine which is always pictured on the back wall of the noh stage is said to have been inspired by this tree, the Yogo Pine at Nara, but it is actually a generic image, a reference to the ritual sakaki tree in the myth of Uzume and Amaterasu, and a representation of the principle of the tree as "conductor" in shamanistic trance possession. Thus the noh drama retains in every presentation an image of its origins.

The image and concept of the sacred tree provide a starting point for a reconstruction of the origin of the noh stage. The ceremonial development of the Shinto religion centers about the *shimboku*, literally "god-tree" or "sacred tree," and "it is the ordinary practice for each shrine to have one tree which is especially venerated" (Holtom, 3). A wooden stand and a fenced-off area for the tree are known as *himorogi*. The earliest *himorogi* were small, rectangular areas of land, "marked at the four corners with bamboo trees, between which strands of shimenawa are hung" (Holtom, 6). The *shimenawa* is the ritual rope which prevented Amaterasu from withdrawing again into her cave, and is used to create a sacred precinct.

> About the purified spot evergreen trees and stones were set up. In this way a taboo area was created wherein the *kami* (gods) might reside more or less permanently and wherein religious rites might be performed with safety.   (Holtom, 6)

The noh stage appears to reproduce the rectangular space of the *himorogi* and to represent the evergreen trees of the surrounding area by the three evergreens marking the *hashigakari*, the passageway to the stage. The stones placed in the surrounding area, or their function, seem to be represented by the white sand strip separating the stage from the spectators. The problem of defining the origins of the noh play is that of reconstructing, within this model of the *himorogi*, more or less exactly what took place there and discerning the manner in which the elements of form and content evolved from shamanistic religious ritual.

I believe that the form and content of the noh play are inseparable and that they cannot be abstracted from the particular nature of the staging. A characteristic or basic noh play may be described as showing the three following typical aspects:

(1) It has, essentially, apart from subsidiary characters, orchestra, chorus, etc., a two-character structure centered upon the performance of the principal actor (*shite*) and a second actor (*waki*), whose function is that of a "bystander" and a "questioner" of the leading performer.

(2) It employs a characteristic convention of travel as a device for

"setting the scene" and creating the situation, and it may use travel passages in other ways. The majority of noh plays begin with the *waki* announcing that he intends to make a journey. He then describes this journey, which may be over vast distances or to some nearby shrine, as if it were taking place. Toward the conclusion, he takes a few steps forward and then returns to his original position, announcing that he has reached his destination. The *waki* is thus established as a stranger in a distant place and able, logically, to question the *shite*, the principal actor, about his identity and about the place in which he finds himself. The convention of travel is inseparable from the role of the *waki* as "questioner." Similar "travel passages" are used in other ways in the noh plays, however, and in a significant number of plays this device provides the situation and action which are basic to the plot, as such.

(3) The content of a characteristic noh play is based upon the manifestation of an apparition. This most often occurs in the second act (or scene) when the *shite*, who appeared as a human in the first act, returns in supernatural form. Two-thirds of all noh plays are of the two-act type. Spirit manifestations are found in a significant number of the one-act type as well, but they are so closely associated with the presentation in terms of an interval which allows for a change of costume that, with Asaji, "we may conclude that a two-act phantasmal play is the proper type of a Noh play" (Asaji, 6).

These three characteristics of a basic noh play are inherent and inseparable; the *waki* travels to the unknown locale where a manifestation of a supernatural being occurs in a transformation of the *shite*'s identity. This inherent pattern derives directly from the nature and form of shamanistic ritual. A similar pattern may be seen in the classic Nine Songs from China of the fourth century B.C. These songs appear, in reconstruction, to be representations of shamanic performances and show both the two-character structure and, most significantly, the origin of the "travel device" used in noh.

The type of shamanism represented in the Nine Songs has striking similarities with the Japanese practice, institutionalized in certain Shinto festivals, in which the shaman, male or female, becomes a temporary consort, a "single-time concubine," for a deity of the opposite sex (Waley, 13–14). The songs show a typical form, a division into two parts. In the first part, the shaman sees the spirit of the deity descending and goes out to meet it. In the second part of each song, the meeting is over and the Spirit has gone; the songs then express a lyrical sadness and a longing for the absent deity. It is thought that in the caesura between these two distinct modes of experience the main ecstatic dance of the shaman was performed. Several of the songs may show a dialogue between two shamans, one bringing down the deity and going out to meet it, and the other representing the deity when it descends (Waley, 60). Arthur Waley feels that the spirit, when its speech is indicated in the songs, may have spoken through the mouth of the actor, just as it did in trance possession, and/or that certain lines were taken by a chorus (Waley, 14–15).

A most significant factor in the Nine Songs is the representation of travel shown in the shaman's departure to meet the descending deity. These travels are described in the first person as if they are occurring in the present to the shaman-actor. The vehicle in which he departs may be a dark cloud, as in Song V.

> Off I ride, borne on a dark cloud!
> May the gusty winds be my vanguard,
> May sharp showers sprinkle the dust!

(Waley, 45)

Or the vehicle may be drawn by a team of horses, and the self-representation that of a drive through changing night and day.

> Now on my balcony falls a ray from Fu-sang,
> I touch my horses and gently drive.
> The night grows pale; now it is broad daylight.

(Waley, 45)

Or the journey may be in a boat, with the performer creating the appropriate representation. As Waley observes, "our shaman in this song is miming the role of someone going out in a boat" (Waley, 31).

> I will deck myself in all my handsome finery
> And set out to find her, riding in my cassia-boat. . . .
>
> I look towards that Princess, but she does not come. . . .
>
> I turn my boat and make for Tung-t'ing.
> My awning is of fig-creeper, bound with basil.
> My paddles of sweet flag, my banners are of orchid.
> I gaze towards the furthest shores of Ts'en-yang.

(Waley, 29)

Strikingly similar travel passages provide the standard opening of a noh play. Consider, for example, the portion of the enactment of travel which begins *Yokihi*. A sorcerer (the *waki*) speaks:

At break of day
I seek a path unknown. . . .

. . . my lord charged me to go quickly forth and find the resting place of her spirit. Above I searched the blue empyrean of Heaven; below, the depths of the Yellow Springs, but nowhere did I learn her spirit's dwelling place. I have not yet been to the Palace of Horai; hence I journey in haste now to Horai, Island of Everlasting Youth.

Be they intimations of darkness,
Would the black arts of sorcery
Bring tidings of the place her spirit dwells!
My ship rides an endless track of sea.
See! Faintly visible, far beyond her sails,
(*He takes a few steps to his right, then returns to his place.*)
An island mountain rises in the mists!
I have reached the Land of Immortality.

(Carl Sesar, trans., Keene [T], 211)

The "sorcerer" follows the patterns of experience of a shaman who undertakes trance travel to the worlds above and below in search of a soul, travels which are characteristic of shamanism. He describes his present travels in the first person, as if they were occurring to him, just as in the Nine Songs. The journey to the "island mountain" retains the quality of the miraculous transposed upon the natural world. Most significant, of course, is the fact that the form of such an opening is typical of the noh play, even when the *waki* is not specifically a "sorcerer." In this example, form and content both reflect their origin in the ritualized trance travel of the shaman.

Ennen noh used travel songs and was, perhaps, entirely based upon the convention of travel. Lombard reproduces the text of *Seeking Jewels in Mount Konron*, which he identifies as an early example of "Pre-Noh-Ennen, of the Tsurane type" (Lombard, 76). The convention of travel is also found in the *dai-furyu* and *sho-furyu* types (O'Neill, 99). The form of the *Seeking Jewels, ennen* noh, in its entirety, is the narration of a journey to Mount Konron. Descriptive, first-person song

alternates between two solo voices and a chorus. This accompanies
dancing which would apparently have enacted the journey.

Solo

We seek a foreign land, three thousand *ri* away;
Through smoky waves on struggling we come.

Chorus

Our native land is distant far, oh, far away;
The mountains crossing, thence we come, we come.
How shall we find again our homeward way?

Solo

Still on and on we go, through valleys dim,
Moon-shadow'd, where never comes the dawn.

(Lombard, 77–78)

Kikushi, reproduced by Lombard as "the sole surviving example of
Dengaku," reveals even more clearly the two-character *waki/shite*
(*tayu*) structure of noh drama and is identical with the *Seeking Jewels*
ennen noh in that it is also comprised entirely of a journey to a "mystic
mountain," here called the Steel-sword Mountain, where a magic elixir
of life is to be found. Mircea Eliade has shown that the "cosmic mountain" and the journey associated with it are characteristic of
shamanism.

> The Abakan Tatars call it "The Iron Mountain" . . . The Mongols
> and the Kalmyk picture it with three or four storeys; the Siberian
> Tatars, with seven; in his mystical journey the Yakut shaman, too,
> climbs a mountain with seven storeys.   (Eliade, 266)

The "mystic mountain" appears in the Nine Songs, and the "island
mountain" in the noh drama *Yokihi* is a variant form of this image. The
"mystic journey," characteristic of *ennen* noh of the *renji* type, is often
to a mountain (Inoura, 58), and this suggests that both the form and
content were based upon the trance travels of shamanic performance.

The *michiyuki* (journey), a "lyrical description of travel in which
names and sites of places are used with poetic effect," is a basic device
in drama, dance, song, and poetry (Araki, 56–57). The *saibara* (a ritual
dance which can also be a *kagura*), the *kusemai*, Buddhist *enkyoku*
("party music"), *kowaka, joruri*, and the *kabuki* are among the forms
based upon or employing *michiyuki*. The very proliferation of modes of
michiyuki attests to a common source and represents, in fact, a transformation in the role of Japanese popular shamanism in which practi-

tioners became directed toward entertainment as such, as dancers, singers, reciters of ballads, etc., so that "Japanese popular entertainment, including Kabuki, emerged in the process of the differentiation of Japanese shamanism" (Hori, 200). Shamanistic influence continued far beyond the time of the formation of noh drama, and the influence of *michiyuki* in dances, I believe, had no more than secondary effect upon it.

The noh drama is so centered upon the *shite* ("performer") that one might feel that it "is exclusively an artistic presentation of the principal actor's acting" (Asaji, 3). Noh is in a sense a monodrama based upon the manifestation of a supernatural being, a god, demon, spirit, etc., aided by a *waki* ("bystander") who serves his function mainly by providing exposition and by asking questions of the "performer." Consideration of the Nine Songs has suggested that the two-character *shite/waki* structure is essentially that of the shaman-helper or deity-shaman relationship in rituals of trance possession. The rituals of Japanese shamanism had precisely this same two-character structure, being composed of a shaman who undertook trance and an assistant who questioned him, made invocations, and sometimes interpreted the information given. These rituals were, in fact, already performances.

In one ritual, for example, the questioner is called the "front seat," and the one who undergoes the trance is called the "middle seat."

> When these teams go into action, the middle seat sits on the ground and in many cases is blindfolded. The front seat sits on the ground in front of and facing the middle seat. The front seat chants and prays invocations, and the middle seat goes into ecstasy. . . . While in ecstasy the middle seat relates the words of the gods, cures the sick, etc.   (Fairchild, 94)

This may be compared with the shamanistic ritual of the powerful Shugendo sect where there is, even more clearly, the nucleus of a noh play (Shugen noh), for it includes a chorus as well as the two-character structure. The chief performer, the master of the ritual, would here correspond with the *waki* in noh, the questioner, fulfilling the same specific, utilitarian function; the possessed individual, chosen for each performance, would correspond with the *shite* in noh.

> There was a chief performer whose duties included overseeing the physical arrangement of the stage, leading the priests and *mikos* in

prayers and invocations, and questioning the possessed individual.
The assistants chanted the invocations to induce the spirits to
possess the individual, and some had the responsibility to subdue
the possessed person if he became violent.   (Fairchild, 88)

Shamanism informed, and was used by, the various religions of Japan.
The first ritual described was of the Ontake Ko sect, which worshiped
Shinto gods but chanted Buddhist sutras and prayers. The ritual of the
syncretic Shugendo sect was usually performed in Buddhist temples.
Both are similar in pattern to rituals developed during the sixth,
seventh, and eighth centuries by the Shinto and Buddhist faiths as a
means of controlling and assimilating the aboriginal clan shamanism. A
"master of worship" undertook trance and was served by a "suppli-
cator" who invoked the presence of the gods and interpreted their
message when they spoke through the possessed person. These rituals
could be accompanied by music, as is the noh play, and they again
show the two-character ritual relationship which was the basis of the
shite-waki structure.

It is apparent that the content of noh, inseparable from its form, also
derives from the rituals of the trance medium. This seems to be an
obvious yet neglected point. O'Neill has briefly sketched the influence
of spirit possession and observed that "it is, indeed, possible that the
'spirit' type of Nō was a direct adaptation of this practice to which was
added, for dramatic purposes, a second act showing the dead person as
he was in life" (O'Neill, 107). However, the "spirit" type of noh drama
is not simply one among many; it is the basic type of noh play. As Asaji
observes, "we may safely say that the Noh drama proper consists in the
phantasmal or visionary plays." The second and only other type, as he
points out, consists of historical or "real life" texts (Asaji, 4). And this
second type of play appears also to have derived from shamanistic
ritual.

The five types of noh drama from which a program of plays is composed, as well as the various subdivisions, may be traced to the same
shamanistic origin. They are:

(1) *Kami noh* or *kami mono* (Divine Pieces), also termed *waki noh*,
    referred to as "god plays."
(2) *Shura noh* or *shura mono* (Battle Pieces); the male play often
    referred to as "warrior plays."
(3) *Katsura noh* or *Katsura mono* (Wig Pieces); the "woman play."

(4) *Zatsu noh* (Miscellaneous Pieces). This group includes *genzi noh* or *genzai mono* (Present Life or Earthly Pieces); *kyoran mono* or *Kuri mono* (Lunatic Pieces); *shura mono* or *onryo mono* (Obsession Pieces); and *yukyo mono* (Enthusiasm Pieces).

(5) *Kiri noh mono* (Final Pieces) which are "demon plays."

(Inoura, 138; Asaji)

These may be compared with the three categories of trance possession characteristic of Japanese popular shamanism as practiced outside organized religion from earliest times to the present day. They are:

(1) *Kami kuchi*, possession by gods or spirits in order to divine, heal the sick, etc.

(2) *Shi kuchi*, possession by the souls of the dead to report conditions, desires, etc., of the dead.

(3) *Iki kuchi*, possession by the souls of the living to obtain information concerning activities, locations, thoughts, etc., of people separated by distance. (based on Fairchild, 55)

The first and fifth categories of noh play can be traced to the manifestations of gods, spirits, and demons associated with the first category of trance possession, *kami kuchi*, with its vital societal functions, particularly that of curing the sick, and to the associated cosmological views. The manifestation of ghosts as spirits of the dead would have originated in the rituals of *shi kuchi*, the second category of trance possession. These plays dominate the second and third categories of noh drama, the male and female plays, and are prominent in the fourth category, the miscellaneous pieces. All five types of noh drama present supernatural apparitions. In fact, the different categories of trance appear to have suggested the categorization of noh play types presented in a program. Subscription performances at the time of Zeami (1363–1443) consisted of three plays, rather than five, and this may have been the original type of program, further indicating a correspondence in this regard.

The only type of play, then, which seems to be different in content from the noh play proper is that in which a well-known contemporary, historical or legendary person, or a humble person such as a madwoman, appears as the principal character. These are the "historical" and "present-life" plays, termed "realistic" because they lack a supernatural manifestation. It is not true, as is often supposed, that they are restricted to the fourth category. In the third category, that of "woman play," we find, for example, *Komachi at Sekidera (Sekidera Komachi)*, which tells of a visit to an old woman whose identity was famous in history. Also in this category, *The Imperial Visit to Ohara (Ohara Goko)* portrays a story derived from a historical episode, the visit of an emperor to a wife from whom conditions have long separated him. In the fourth category, miscellaneous plays, we have comparable examples: *Semimaru*, in which a madwoman visits her blind brother, and *The Reed Cutter (Ashikari)*, in which a woman searches for and finds her husband in a distant locality.

All four plays are based on the convention of travel to a distant locale. They differ hardly at all from the "spirit type" of noh, lacking only the transformation into a supernatural being. It may be postulated, therefore, that the so-called realistic plays derive from the third category of trance possession, *iki kuchi*, possession of the shaman not by a supernatural being but by the soul of a living person who is distant, in order to know his location, state of affairs, etc. And indeed, the typical or standard situation in such plays is one of family members long separated by distance.

Very often, the condition of the protagonist in these plays would approximate the state of trance, when the medium "speaks in strange voices, becomes excited and slightly crazed, and goes into ecstasy, her body quivering and shaking" (Fairchild, 62). Madwoman plays (Lunatic or Obsession Pieces) and Enthusiasm Pieces of the fourth category would have this basis in the characteristics of ecstasy. The episode of insanity provides a dramatic climax comparable with spirit manifestation and is based on dances derived from shamanism. It is caused by separation from loved ones, as in *Rodaiko (The Drum of the Prison and the Woman)*, *Hyakuman (The Insane Mother Hyakuman at Saga)*, *Kashiwazaki (The Lady of Kashiwazaki)*, and other plays. Both the ecstasy of trance and the specific function of "present life" trance contact with persons living at a distance have been given dramatic representation. A related use of the characteristics of trance performance is that in which the possessing spirit or person manifest is a famous dancer or "sorceress," as in *Eguchi (The Courtesans of Eguchi)*, *Futari Shizuka (Two Shizukas, The Dancing Girls)*, *Higaki (The Woman within the Cypress Fence)*, *Aoi No Ue (Lady Aoi Possessed)*, and other plays. Even when there is no spirit manifestation, these plays are not actually "realistic," but show the assimilation of myth, legend, and literary material to a basic ritual pattern of trance mediumship. The "ecstatic" plays with women protagonists found in the fourth category as well as the "woman plays" of the third category would seem to be based upon the importance of woman practitioners in Japanese shamanism, the *miko*, "priests, soothsayers, magicians, prophets and shamans in the folk religion, and . . . the chief performers in organized Shintoism" (Fairchild, 57).

The development of noh drama from trance rituals was not simply fortuitous. There must always be reasons for the transposition of an actualizing, effective ritual into representation and mimetic enactment, however charged the noh might be with the spirit of trance performance. The societal pressures which produced the noh play began, it would seem, with the official decrees, issued in A.D. 780 and A.D. 807, which prohibited ecstasy outside the shrines, primarily as a means of combating the spread of Buddhism. These decrees created an outcast class of the *mikos* and related practitioners of shamanic trance, but had little effect upon their popularity other than directing them toward the performance of dances and songs as entertainment. The insistence of the authorities and the ineffectiveness of the decrees may be estimated, in part, from the fact that they continued to be renewed and issued regularly until 1873, when ecstasy was banned from the Shinto religion entirely (Fairchild, 53). Two different but complementary situations for the transposition of ritual into drama are thus suggested. By eliminating the functional aspects of the ritual, such as curing, divination, etc., which were dependent upon the trance, but not the representational and dramatic aspects of the ritual, plays could still be performed by the various sects outside the precincts of their shrines. Such proselytizing by the sects was common religious practice. For those who had become outcasts but still sought to earn a living from their shamanistic abilities, dramatization of the rituals as entertainment, with function and trance eliminated, would likewise have been a logical response to the situation of proscription. It would appear that the various types of noh drama developed independently, both within the sects and outside their direct influence, from related types of shamanistic ritual which had been placed under interdiction.

In order to transpose the specifically personal and socially effective functions of shamanic ritual into a generalized, representational performance mode, the artists of *saragaku* noh turned to the classics of literature and history for their material. The ghosts or souls of distant persons invoked in ritual for specific individuals became, in a logical substitution, those of persons known or relevant to an audience from their appearance in literature or history. (The present-day Chinese medium incarnates such persons in trance rituals for the same reasons.) The anecdotes of *Kojandan, The Tale of Genji, Heike Monogatari*, and many other classical sources were used, this work made all the more remarkable by the sustained artistry with which the form of ritual was preserved.

The whole range of formal, highly refined aesthetic principles characteristic of the noh drama was directly associated with the rituals in which the form had its origin. These rituals were already highly formal and evidenced the principles of taste and refinement. Even when *miko* trance possession was repeated again and again on the same day, the procedure could not be altered, nor could additions or omissions be made (Fairchild, 85). The precision of ritual movement and form was directly associated with a verbal refinement. The *kami*, the gods who spoke through the shaman, had to be represented in beautiful speech.

> Related to the notion of *mi-koto* (divine words of the kami) was the belief in *koto-dama* (the potency of the spirit of *tama* residing in the spoken words). Beautifully phrased speech and correctly uttered words were believed to bring about good results, while carelessly phrased speech and incorrectly pronounced words were believed to bring about evil results.   (Kitagawa, 18)

To the ritual refinement of gesture and speech we may add the beauty of music, for "the state of ecstasy known as kami-possession . . . was often induced by the playing of the *koto* and other musical instruments" (Kitagawa, 19). These remained as principles when literary passages were incorporated into noh texts, but they are not factors which, of themselves, modified a primitive form. Like the form and content of noh drama, an aesthetic of beauty bespeaks its specific origins in ritual.

In conclusion I return, then, to an important earlier point, the mirror in the myth of Amaterasu understood as a shamanistic device for inducing trance. Such a mirror is found as a key property in *Shokun (Wan Chao-Chun Sacrificed)*, a drama performed by all schools of noh, where its presence "points to an earlier form of drama" (Keene [T], 166). The ghost of a woman is summoned to appear in the mirror, just as she would have appeared there to the shaman in trance, and the travel to the woman and the manifestation of a supernatural being are accomplished on stage through this device. The noh theatre itself has, as a basic property, a mirror which seems to relate to the same ritual function.

The *Kagami-No-Ma*, the "room of the mirror," is a special room opening onto the bridge to the stage, where the actors who wear masks, particularly the *shite*, traditionally prepare themselves by deep concentration before the mirror prior to entering. "Once a Noh actor has put on his mask his whole body and soul seems to take on the character of the personage he represents" (Toki, 34). Form and content of the noh are one. The heritage of trance possession, exercised in terms of a concentrated artistry, may be summarized, perhaps, in Zeami's phrase, "the spirit of noh."

Chapter V

GREECE:
THE FORMS OF DIONYSUS

Ancient Greek tragedy and a certain type of comedy called the satyr play made their first "official" appearance together, or nearly so, at the Athenian festival of the City Dionysia in 534 B.C., founded in honor of Dionysus Melanaegis (Dionysus of the Black Aegis, a shield, perhaps a goatskin), also called Dionysus Eleuthereus. A statue of the god had been brought to Athens from the city of Eleutherai to commemorate an episode in which the daughters of the eponymous Eleuther had been driven mad by the god. Performances of another type of comedy, identified with Aristophanes and the "old comedy," made their first appearance at the City Dionysia almost fifty years later, in 486 B.C. The question of the origins of these three forms of drama has provided scholarship with a source of apparently endless and inconclusive debate.

A basic hypothesis, to be developed in the following pages, would be that the three forms of drama originated in the dithyramb as circular choruses danced and sung to the music characteristic of Dionysianism. Tragedy, we know, began, as Aristotle tells us, with "the leaders of the dithyramb." Thespis, it is said, added a prologue and a set speech, but there was only a chorus and a single actor for the some sixty-two years of performances of tragedy until Aeschylus added a second actor about 472 B.C. This fact is of paramount importance; in its origin and for more than sixty-two years, tragedy was a choral performance of the dithyramb-plus-actor, not drama as interaction between persons. There is

90

reason to believe that the supposed originator of tragedy, Thespis, was a mythologized personage, his name derived from the adjective *thespis* meaning "inspired," as combined with "song" or "singer" in passages of the *Odyssey* (Pickard-Cambridge, 72). The word itself suggests the ecstatic or Dionysian nature of tragedy. In regard to Thespis, it is not of much use to speculate on how long tragedy as dithyramb-plus-actor antedated 534 B.C. However, something curiously like it occurred some sixty-five years earlier, about 600 B.C. At that time, the Suda lexicon says that Arion of Methymna, a lyric poet, "invented the tragic mode and first composed a stationary chorus and sung a dithyramb and named what the chorus sang and introduced satyrs speaking verses," and other scholia support the attribution to him of tragedy arrived at through innovation in the dithyramb (Pickard-Cambridge, 97–98).

It is to this point in time that our current problems in regard to the origins of tragedy and its relationship to comedy seem most clearly to return. They stem from Aristotle's observation that tragedy derived from comedy. Because tragedy "changed from *satyric* [comedy's] small plots and laughable diction were solemnized late" to become tragedy (Pickard-Cambridge, 89); or, said in another way, "short incidents and the language of ridicule developed in length and dignity as the satyr-play changed into tragedy" (Grube, 9). This is difficult to accept literally. The basic dithyramb, as will be considered, was an ecstatic trance-dance. There is no reason to believe that it had to pass through comedy, in the form of a satyr play, before it again became serious. Literally, the satyr play didn't change into anything; it continued to exist in its own mode. Since we then must be considering influence, there are two important ways in which comedy, as a dithyramb performed by satyrs, appears to have influenced the serious, lyric, and ecstatic dithyramb. The first, cited by Aristotle, was a change in meter from tetrameter to iambic, "when speech came in." We note that Arion introduced satyrs speaking verses, not singing them, and the satyrs might previously also have been comic performers. The second, stated by Aristotle simply as "the number of scenes," would seem to relate directly to introduction of the second and third actors in the tragic dithyramb, clearly a means of facilitating the playing of a number of scenes. It seems most likely, considering the nature of comedy, that the satyr play moved from the strictly choral form sooner, and that it had three actors throughout the some sixty-seven years of Dionysia performance that it took to add the second and third actors to the tragic dithyramb. The only extant satyr play, Euripides' *Cyclops*, dated about

423 B.C., shows that its form was then like that of tragedy, with three actors and a similar use of the chorus. In this sense, tragedy as dramatic action was "solemnized late," though it is a regrettable phrase.

For a long time, scholars attempted to associate tragedy with a satyr chorus by deriving the word *tragoidia* from *tragos*, meaning "goat." But the satyrs were horse-men, not goat-men. It is now observed that a meaning of "song of goats" is linguistically impossible (Else, 25) and that any derivation from "singers dressed in goat-skins" can be safely discarded (Pickard-Cambridge, 124). Webster thinks it might mean "singer at the goat-sacrifice" or "singer for the goat-prize" (Pickard-Cambridge, 123). Jane Ellen Harrison suggested that the word derived from the name for a cereal, a type of spelt, known as "the goat" (Harrison [P], 420). She later retracted this, although it continued to please Robert Graves, apparently because of the affinity with vegetation theory. The point is that such variants are possible, to the extent that they no longer mean "goat."

The word *komos* or *komus* from which the designation for comedy derives, sounded like the word for "village," so early commentators said comedy came from the village, just as they said tragedy meant dancing around a goat or for a goat prize. The actual meaning of the word *komus* is unknown, and it may not be of Hellenic origin. The meaning of dithyramb is not known, but the word is not of Hellenic origin. Perhaps it would be best not to overtax the abilities of philology in attempting to associate "tragedy" with "goat." If the satyrs, who were horse-men not goat-men, were instrumental in the creation of tragedy, as they most probably were, they soon went their own way into satire. More importantly, they were trance dancers, as we shall see.

The Kuretes and Korybantes represented basic types of the trance-dance complex which was characteristic of Dionysianism. From them, or from the modes which evolved from them, such as the ecstatic dithyramb, we may trace the origins of tragic drama. In mythological terms, the Kuretes and Korybantes were thought of not only as the etiological foundation of the trance-dance complex but of the Greek religion itself. The chorus of maenads in Euripides' *Bacchae* speaks of this as follows:

And I praise the holies of Crete,
the caves of the dancing Curetes,
there where Zeus was born,
where helmed in triple tier

around the primal drum
the Corybantes danced. They,
they were the first of all
whose whirling feet kept time
to the strict beat of the taut hide
and the squeal of the wailing flute.
Then from them to Rhea's hands
the holy drum was handed down;
but, stolen by the raving Satyrs,
fell at last to me and now
accompanies the dance
which every other year
celebrates your name:
   Dionysus!
          (120-34, Arrowsmith; trans., Grene and Lattimore, 166)

The passage describes an etiological sequence in which the "primal drum" was passed from one trance-dance group to another. The satyrs are one of these. The Korybantes (or Corybantes), however, were not Cretan, but were of Thraco-Phrygian origin. Their name meant "whirlers" (Rose, 171), which would associate them with a well-known means of inducing trance, both shamanistic and Middle Eastern. Guthrie observes that "to 'korybant' served as a verb in Greek, meaning to be in a state of ecstasy or divine madness in which hallucinations were possible" (Guthrie, 118). There seems to have been a "Korybantic malady," common in Phrygia and apparently similar to maenadism.

> Those affected by such fevers saw strange figures that corresponded
> to no objective reality, and heard the sound of invisible flutes, until
> at last they were excited to the highest pitch of frenzy and were
> seized with a violent desire to dance.   (Rohde, 286)

Mythologically, the Korybantes were the "attendants" of Kybele, the Phrygian goddess identified with the rites of Dionysus in the *Bacchae* (78ff.). We will show that the rites of Attis, associated with Kybele, were shamanistic, and this basis is further indicated in H. J. Rose's summary of the nature and function of the Korybantes.

> ... they are constantly associated with ritual dancing, with mys-
> teries and magical cures; the latter it seems were taught only to

women. Here again it seems not impossible that behind all lie the figures of very old medicine-men, dancers, like the Roman Salii, of sacred dances and performers of magic, and deified in process of time.

(Rose, 171)

The Korybantes and the Kuretes were apparently so much alike that the names came to be used interchangeably. The best known information in regard to the latter is the Song of the Kuretes preserved in fragments found on Crete. The type of inscription used places it quite late, in the third century A.D., but attempts have been made to date it earlier. The vegetation concept of Harrison's *Themis* was based upon Gilbert Murray's translation of this song, which reads as follows:

Io, Kouros most Great, I give thee hail, Kronian, Lord of all that is wet and gleaming, thou art come at the head of thy Daimones. To Dikte for the Year, Oh, march, and rejoice in the dance and song,
That we make to thee with harps and pipes mingled together, and sing as we come to a stand at thy well-fenced altar.
Io, etc.
For here the shielded Nurturers took thee, a child immortal, from Rhea, and with noise of beating feet hid thee away.
Io, etc. . . .

And the Horai began to be fruitful year by year (?) and Dike to possess mankind, and all wild living things were held about by wealth-loving Peace.
Io, etc. . . .

To us also leap for full jars, and leap for fleecy flocks, and leap for fields of fruit, and for hives to bring increase.
Io, etc. . . .

Leap for our Cities, and leap for our sea-borne ships, and leap for our young citizens and for goodly Themis.

(Harrison [T], 7–8)

The intention was to consider the dance a fertility ritual, and the translation appears to have been forced and misinterpreted for that purpose. Nilsson pointed out in 1927 that the operative words should be read literally, as they stand, with the meaning leap *into*, not supplied with meaning from a derived, secondary form signifying leap *on behalf of* (Nilsson, 478). Joseph Fontenrose's 1966 critique of ritual theory supplemented the text with other fragments that have been discovered, and he arrived at the same conclusion in regard to translation. The meaning of the words in question must be read as "into"; " 'To us' must be stricken, the 'full jars' become herds of cattle, the 'hives' become houses, and Themis is renowned rather than goodly" (Fontenrose, 29). To support belief in fertility ritual, interpretation as well as text had been forced, since the verses were thought to call upon the god to leap as the dancers did, thus representing the "sympathetic magic" involved in vegetation ritual as the Frazerian school understood the basic principle to be. This is far from a satisfactory concept of ritual practices. The significant point, however, is that the verses originate in the mode of the trance dance. They call upon the spirit of the god to leap *into* the cattle, the houses, the ships, etc., into all the forms of the surrounding world, as into the dancers. They call down illumination; they do not invoke procreation.

In etiological myth, the Kuretes and the Korybantes were associated with the origins of the religion as such. The Kuretes were said to have protected the infant Zeus, while the Korybantes were sometimes said to have performed the same function in regard to the infant Dionysus. These are clearly metaphors of origin. The trance dances guarded and "nourished" the infancy of the concepts that found configuration in the worship of Zeus and Dionysus. It was sometimes said that the "infant Zeus" was guarded by the Kuretes with a clashing of shields, and sometimes, as in the Song of the Kuretes, that his cries were disguised and hidden by the sounds of the dancers' beating feet. The first image suggests an exorcism, with arms taken up against supernatural powers. But the Korybantes were women, or principally women. The image of shields seems to be based on metaphor. That is, the trance and the trance-dance itself were the "shield" that protected the "infant deity," and "his" cries were those of the dancers themselves in participation in the phenomenon from which the religion was born and around which its conceptual religious structure formed.

One function of trance dance in the ancient world was exorcistic, as represented by the troupe of dancers imported into Rome in 361 B.C. to alleviate a pestilence. That Gilbert Murray referred to their function as "a sort of Fertility Charm," epitomizes the devious logic and doubtful conclusions that have characterized ritual theory (Murray [R], 46).

Apotropaic dances against disease are certainly "a sort of magic." Dances to exorcise forces harmful to crops, if they were practiced at all, and of which we have no evidence concerning ancient Greece, were also "a sort of magic," but they were not the basis of the function.

Contrary to general belief, Dionysus was not a vegetation or fertility god, and there is virtually nothing in any of Greek mythology that suggests that he was. The earliest reference to him, found in Homer, calls him "mad Dionysus" (*Iliad*, 13.143). Other myths say that he was driven mad by Hera and that he himself drove others mad—Pentheus; Agave and her sisters; Lycurgus; Boutes; the daughters of Minyas; the daughters of Proetus; the daughters of Eleuther; the pirates who captured him; and so on. The name of his women followers, the maenads, meant "madwomen." He was associated with the *effect* of wine, as a means of producing religious ecstasy, and with the *effect* of ivy, which was an intoxicant and was chewed by the maenads to induce an ecstatic state. Dionysus was the god of insanity and of catharsis. This may be observed as the basic function of "maenadism," and studied in terms of the uses and symbolism of ivy which characterized Dionysianism.

> For women possessed by Bacchic frenzies rush straightway for ivy and tear it to pieces, clutching it in their hands and biting it with their teeth; so that not altogether without plausibility are they who assert that ivy, possessing as it does an exciting and distracting breath of madness, deranges persons and agitates them, and in general brings on a wineless drunkenness and joyousness in those that are precariously disposed toward spiritual exaltation.
>
> Wherefore it is excluded from the ritual of the Olympian gods, nor can any ivy be seen in the temple of Hera at Athens, or in the temple of Aphrodite at Thebes; but it has its place in the Agrionia and the Nyctelia, the rites of which are for the most part performed at night.   (Plutarch, *The Roman Questions*, 291 A,B)

This observation pertaining to an age of syncretistic religion would be of less value if ivy were not a basic symbolism in Dionysian myth. From there its funtion in the behavior of the maenads can be reconstructed.

First, the origin of ivy, according to myth, was that it appeared simultaneously with the birth of Dionysus in order to shield him from the lightning that destroyed his mother, Semele. In the *Bacchae*, the still-smoking tomb of Semele is covered with vines that are most probably ivy, and it was Dionysus who thus "screened her grave" with the vines. An Orphic Hymn describes the role of ivy in the prevention of the destruction of the palace of Pentheus when it was struck by earth-quake and lightning, as in the *Bacchae*. Ivy "is supposed to have wrapped itself around everything and to have checked the shocks of the earthquakes which accompanied the lightning bolts" (Otto, 153). This can only mean, quite literally, that ivy was supposed to have sustained, preserved, or held integrated the "ground" of the mind, and to have checked the shock to the structure of personality in an episode of insanity.

Identification of the lightning bolt with the tree and pillar as representations of the vertical axis associated with Dionysus was the reason why an ivy-twined column was held sacred to this god by the Thebans, and why he was known as "the one who is entwined around pillars" (Otto, 153). Ivy was also twined about the thyrsus, the staff used in Dionysian worship, indicating it to have been thought of in an identical sense, as a "conductor" of "illumination" in religious experience. Dionysus as ivy protected the Power; he could cause insanity or cure it.

Symbolizing the spirit of Dionysus, ivy was essentially an image of the "entangling growth" of delusion and hallucination that creates around one its own particular darkness, the enclosed dark space that phenomenology calls the "tomb world" of psychosis. Thus, and with this meaning, ivy sprang up in the apartments of the daughters of Eleuther to represent their madness when they saw a "vision" of Diony-sus, a hallucinatory image of the god they had refused to worship. In a similar manner, when Dionysus had been kidnapped by pirates, it was said that he caused ivy to grow up suddenly about them, entangling and enshrouding the operations of the ship, and that he then changed the culprits into dolphins. The maenads described by Plutarch, then, were attempting to break out of the enclosing "dark space" of the "tomb world" of insanity by rending the ivy as if it were the enclosure. Amok, one of the fugue states similar to maenadism, is characterized by a sudden, unmotivated murder spree, and those who have "gone amok" and survived have described "a feeling of blackening of eyesight from which they tried to slash their way out" (Arieti, 557). The breaking out of an enclosing darkness represented by the ivy seems to have been an ecstatic ritual devised as a symbolic surrogate, as a "release," and as a cathartic protection of sanity. Irwin Rohde noted in general terms the development of the concept of catharsis that was central to Dionysianism.

We hear of a "Bakis" who "purified" and delivered the women of Sparta from an attack of madness that has spread like an epidemic among them. The prophetic age of Greece must have seen the origin of what later became part of the regular duties of the "seer": the cure of diseases, especially those of the mind; the averting of evil of every kind by various strange means, and particularly the supply of help and counsel by "purifications" of a religious nature. The gift or art of prophecy, the purification of "the unclean," the healing of disease, all seem to be derived from one source. Nor can we be long in doubt as to what the single source of this threefold capacity must have been. The world of invisible spirits surrounding man, which ordinary folk know only by its effects, is familiar and accessible to the ecstatic prophet, the *Mantis*, the spirit-seer. As exorcist he undertakes to heal disease; the *Kathartic* process is also essentially and originally an exorcism of the baleful influences of the spirit world.   (Rohde, 294)

These are the functions and heritage of shamanism as it was manifest in ancient Greece. Dionysus Eleuthereus, the god of the City Dionysia, was associated with apotropaic and curative functions, and the introduction of his image also caused disease. "In Athens, as in some other places in Greece, the god was not well received, and the men of Athens were smitten with a disease from which (it was said) they only freed themselves (on the advice of an oracle) by manufacturing *phalloi* in honor of the god" (Pickard-Cambridge [F], 57). We will have reason to consider the apotropaic function of the phallus later. For the moment, let us consider the postulate that the function of catharsis in ritual trance dances led directly to the understanding of the function of tragedy as expressed in Aristotle's famous definition that "through pity and fear it achieves the purgation (catharsis) of such emotions" (*Poetics*, 1449C).

Gerald Else has shaped a theory which has met with some attention in which he holds that the dithyramb performed at the City Dionysia was "the literary dithyramb as Arion had shaped it" and that tragedy had some other source than the ecstatic dithyramb, since it was characterized by *logos*, which "is not only un-dithyrambic and un-Dionysiac, it is anti-Dionysiac" (Else, 74, 69). I will later sketch how Orphism, an "anti-Dionysiac" movement within Dionysianism, did indeed bring *logos* to bear in a transformation of the ecstatic dithyramb. But it cannot be shown that Arion's "literary" dithyramb was an "un-ecstatic," for Pindar's certainly was not, nor can the origin of the "literary" modes of performance in ancient Greece be neatly separated

from the ecstatic. Plato (*Ion* 534 AB) made this observation in regard
to lyric poets:

> Just as the Korybantian worshippers do not dance when in their
> senses, so the lyric poets do not compose those beautiful songs in
> their senses, but when they have started on the melody and rhythm
> they begin to be frantic; and it is under possession, as the Bacchants
> are possessed and not in their senses when they draw honey and
> milk from the rivers, that the soul of the lyric poet does the same
> thing, by their own report.

To Else's view that Arion's dithyramb was somehow suddenly "un-
Dionysian" because it was "literary," we may oppose the concept of
Werner Jaeger, based on an extensive knowledge of ancient literary
modes, who judged that the choral dithyramb had originated "when a
poet realized that dithyrambic ecstasy provided a spiritual tension
which could be translated into art" (Jaeger, 249–50). He associated this
spiritual tension with the effect upon an audience, with the reason for
the condensation of tragedy into "one fateful moment," and with the
characteristic of lofty, imaginative language,

> . . . which reached its highest emotional tension when supported by
> the rhythm of dance and music in the dithyrambic ecstasy of the
> choruses. By deliberately avoiding the vocabulary and syntax of
> ordinary language, it transported the audience to a world of higher
> reality.   (Jaeger, 248–49)

The choral dithyramb-plus-actor of early tragedy achieved its effect by
a fusion of elevated, literary images (*logos*, if you will) and ecstasy. The
tragic aesthetic must have been achieved, as it was in later tragedy, by
choice of those moments in which the chorus, composed of fifty members, was gripped in turn by a series of powerful emotions: fear, pity,
hope, pathos.

> It was naturally impossible, then, for early tragedy to represent a
> realistic series of events with lifelike details. The chorus was entirely
> unfitted for such a task. All that it could attempt was to become a
> perfect instrument of the varied emotions called out by the plot,
> and to express them in song and dance. The poet could make full
> use of the limited possibilities of this instrument only by intro-

ducing several violent and sudden changes in the course of the
events described by the plot, so as to draw from the chorus a wide
range of contrasting types of expression.   (Jaeger, 250)

Having avoided considering the chorus by labeling it "literary," Else
observes that "the actor's speeches, as we first glimpse them in Aeschylus, are not spoken as if by one possessed, but on the contrary in a
sober, rational, even pedantic style, without a trace of frenzy" (Else,
69). A single example can serve to remind us of another view, another
"hearing" of the plays.

> An echo of such daimonic possession, and of the horrible reality
> and terror that it had for the possessed, can still be heard in the
> cries and convulsions which Aeschylus in the *Agamemnon* gives to
> his Kassandra—a true picture of the primitive Sibyl, and a type that
> the poets of that prophetic generation had reflected backwards into
> the earlier past of legend.   (Rohde, 293)

How many other examples of tone and character could we cite to
support a rather traditional view that Greek tragedy was not "un-
Dionysiac"? It strove through a representation of pity and terror for a
catharsis that was in fact based upon ritual concepts and practices still
present in the Dionysian worship to which the performances were
dedicated.

An understanding of the origins of ancient Greek theatre, of tragedy,
comedy, and satyr play, cannot be arrived at without an understanding
of Dionysus and of Dionysian worship. Dionysus was the god of an
ancient shamanism, and his rituals were essentially cathartic and apotropaic. To establish this concept in detail, it is necessary to examine the
myths of Dionysus and, quite literally, to disentangle them from interpretation which would see them as representations of "vegetation
rituals" which are alleged to have formed the basis of comedy and
tragedy. This seems particularly necessary in view of the fact that Professor T. B. L. Webster has chosen to present vegetation theory concepts as a basis for drama in his updating and revision of the standard
text on the ancient theatre, the 1927 edition of *Dithyramb Tragedy
and Comedy* by Arthur Pickard-Cambridge, which has been called "the
classic treatment of the subject not only in English but in any language,

in the sense of a truly critical review of the evidence and judgment of what it is worth and what it indicates" (Else, 108). Pickard-Cambridge had found neither evidence for the existence of the so-called *eniautos daimon* vegetation rituals of death-and-resurrection alleged to have been practiced in ancient Greece nor significant traces of these rituals as they were supposed to have been preserved in tragedy, according to the theory of Gilbert Murray, or in comedy, as proposed by Francis Macdonald Cornford. Professor Webster chose to abridge the careful analyses of these topics and to present vegetation theory again in a more general way that would almost seem to bypass any need for direct evidence. He agreed that Cornford's theory of comedy "clearly does not work when applied in detail to the plays of Aristophanes," but it was still "suggestive and valuable," since Dionysus was "a god of vegetation and all his festivals were therefore vegetation festivals," so that "comedy certainly was vegetation ritual." Murray's theory of tragedy, although lacking any proof, was likewise "tenable and valuable." Both comedy and tragedy derived from a "rhythm" which had been established by vegetation ritual of the *eniautos daimon* type in the Mycenaean age (1580–1120 B.C.). The opponents of Dionysus in the myths about him were based on personified forces that were the opponents of the vegetation exorcists, as we might call them, in the ritual.

> The ritual is designed to overcome the forces of nature which resist the new growth of vegetation, but in story this resistance is translated into the resistance of human kings to the worship of Dionysus and his maenads, such as the Pentheus story in Thebes, the Proitos story and the Perseus story in Argos, the Erigone story in Attica, and other stories located in Orchomenos and Eleutherai.
>
> (Pickard-Cambridge, 128–29)

To the contrary, it can be shown that these stories were based upon a symbolism derived from shamanism. First, however, I would like to review the evidence that has been used to support the belief that Dionysus was a vegetation god and a god of the year-cycle. The standard, often-cited references are found in two passages in Plutarch dating from the first century A.D. and four lines of poetry by the Christian Rhetor, Himerius, dating from the fourth century A.D. There is little else, if anything. In one passage, Plutarch cites two lines purportedly from Pindar that run:

May gladsome Dionysus swell the fruit upon the trees,
The hallowed splendour of harvest-time.

(Isis and Osiris, 35)

I believe that Plutarch's comment upon these lines elsewhere (*Moralia*, 348) is sufficient and apt criticism in regard to relevance that should be attached to them.

> He showed [this poem] to Corinna, but she laughed and said that one should sow with the hand, not with the whole sack. For in truth Pindar had confused and jumbled together a seed-mixture, as it were, of myths, and poured them into his poem.

The second passage from Plutarch (*Isis and Osiris*, 69) is famous as evidence for the belief that Dionysus was a god of the year-cycle.

> The Phrygians, believing that the god is asleep in the winter and awake in the summer, sing lullabies for him in the winter and in the summer chants to arose him, after the manner of Bacchic worshippers. The Paphlagonians assert that in the winter he is bound fast and imprisoned, but that in the spring he bestirs himself and sets himself free again.

Harrison apparently did not feel that "lullabies" were appropriate to the Bacchic worshipers, and translated the key phrase as "they celebrate to him Bacchic revels, which in winter are Goings to Sleep, and in summer Wakings-up" (Harrison [T], 179). The worth of these folk tales as reflection of what more the gods might represent or mean is inadequate. Religion in this period had lost awareness of earlier beliefs and practices and was extremely syncretistic and confused. Plutarch, for example, identified Dionysus with Osiris; with Serapis, the Egyptian god of healing; and with Pluto, the Roman god of the underworld. Osiris, he believed, was a Greek god. Pans and satyrs, he said, had given the warning that Typhon had shut Osiris in the chest, but he drew the line at the people who said that Typhon had fled from battle for seven days mounted on the back of an ass and then fathered two sons named Hierosolymus and Judaeus. Such people, he said, "are manifestly, as the very names show, attempting to drag Jewish traditions into the legend" (*Isis and Osiris*, 31).

Martin Nilsson, who wanted to believe in Dionysus as a god of the year-cycle, observed in 1927 in regard to the Plutarch passages that:

> ... the authenticity of this information may be questioned, since it occurs in an Egyptianized discussion of the identity of Dionysus and Osiris. ... In this age of syncretism, which very seriously affected the mysteries, we have always to reckon with an introduction of foreign elements and ideas.   (Nilsson, 493)

Rather than abandon the idea of Dionysus as a vegetation god, Nilsson postulated two separate types of Dionysian worship. One had an origin in Thrace, and since its observances were restricted to the winter it worshiped a Dionysus who "cannot be a representative of vegetation." Another cult, he said, had its origin in Asia Minor and worshiped a "spirit of vegetation" that "vanishes during winter and revives in spring" (Nilsson, 498). The only evidence to support belief in this second cult was a few lines of extremely flowery poetry from Himerius (A.D. 310–390) that appear to cite Lydian practices of some kind. They mention bacchantes and the spring. They are later than Plutarch, as poetic as Pindar, and I doubt that they are at all meaningful.

Let us consider another fiction, a fabrication of vegetation theory, that Professor Webster suggests should still be taken seriously. This involves Lewis Farnell's interpretation of a legend from Eleutherae concerned with Dionysus of the Black Aegis, in which, according to Webster, "he finds evidence of a ritual duel between Xanthos and Melanthos, 'fair man and black man,' which (following Usener) he interprets with great probability as 'a special form of the old-world ritual fight between winter and summer or spring' " (Pickard-Cambridge, 120). Webster goes on to cite Farnell's description of how the play might have spread through the villages of Greece. Usener's study, published in the *Archiv Für Religionswissenschaft* of 1904, was cited by Murray and by Cornford as evidence of the combat or *agon* that served as an element in their hypothetical ritual series. Since it had been pointed out that this "ritual" had no chorus, George Thomson agreed that it must lie off the direct line of descent to tragedy, but felt both that it was "the stuff of which tragedy was made" and that it "would lend itself to boisterous treatment," and could have been the origin of comedy (Thomson, 169). Even H. D. F. Kitto, in a paper of 1960 in which he referred to ritual theory as "modern moonshine," assumed that there is a record of a "ritual and mimetic fight" at Eleutherae and that "it is likely enough that this represents the triumph of a winter-spirit over the summer-spirit" (Kitto, 6, 18).

The account on which this fabrication has been based is given by the Scholiast on Aristophanes. This has been translated by William Ridgeway.

> War broke out between the Athenians and the Boeotians for the possession of Celaenae, a place on their borders. Xanthus, the Boeotian, challenged the Athenian king Thymoetes. When the latter declined the challenge, Melanthus, a Messenian (of the race of Periclymenus, the son of Neleus), then living at Athens, took up the challenge with an eye to obtaining the kingdom. When they met in single combat Melanthus saw someone behind Xanthus clad in the skin of a he-goat, that is, a black goatskin (*aegis*), and he cried out that it was not fair for him to bring a second. The other looked behind, and Melanthus at once struck him and slew him. In consequence of this the festival of the Apaturia and of Dionysus Melanaegis was established.   (Ridgeway [O], 75–76)

This is all we have. It is apparent that it is a legend based on an event that happened once or was supposed to have happened and that it does not represent a "mimetic" combat. There is not the slightest scrap of evidence to suggest that this combat was then repeated as a ritual or "mumming," so it makes little sense to talk about whether it had three actors or two, etc. The trick or ruse appears to be just that, but it relates to other "apparitions" of Dionysus, most of which cause insanity, as we shall see. There is nothing in the legend to suggest that the situation or the names of the characters relate in any way to a "battle between the seasons." Even in those terms, we note that Melanthos (black man) is the victor, which runs counter to the theory, since he would supposedly represent evil and the "old year."

In order to establish a relationship to the ritual pattern, it was necessary for Usener, who had originally introduced the theory, to (1) associate the legendary figures with gods and (2) indicate some connection between the hypothetical ritual and the vegetation cycle.

This was done as follows. Suidas, an encyclopaedist of the tenth century A.D. referencing Polybius of the second century B.C., had preserved, according to Usener, "a few words that are worth their weight in gold" (Usener, 302). These few words of Polybius told of a mock-battle or tournament of armored cavalry held by the Macedonian army in the month of Xandikos, in the spring. In the same month, an important civic festival or feast, called the Xandika, was known to have been held. It is far from clear that there was any connection between the mock-battle staged as a "purification" of the army and the civic festival, although Usener assures us they were "closely connected" (Usener: 302). It is clear, however, that there is no connection between the mock-combat engaged in by armored Macedonian horsemen and the alleged ritual inferred from the Greek legend. It has been assumed that they had a name, Xanthos, in common. The necessary connection between the festival Xandica, the cavalry tournament and the month named Xandikos was made by Usener by (1) supposing that "the great festival . . . has given its name to the Macedonian month Xandikos," and (2) that "back of the feast of Xandika and the similarly derived month-name stands a god, but a god downgraded to a hero, and he is named Xanthos" (Usener, 303). It would be more reasonable, and even more likely, to suppose that the month was named "fair" because it was in spring, that the name of the festival derived from the name of the month in which it was celebrated, and that no god or hero was involved at all.

The names Xanthos and Melanthos and their cognates, as associated with the meanings "fair" and "dark" or "blond" and "brunet," were common enough, and were applied as names for rivers and localities, among their varied uses. No Melanthos is mentioned in the Macedonian material, and it seems apparent that no one named Xanthos was either. The mock cavalry combat was not a manifestation of the alleged battle between the seasons, and it had no association, direct or otherwise, with the combat in the legend. There is nothing to support the belief that the figures in the legend were once gods who had been downgraded to the status of heroes. To sustain this view Usener suggested, in effect, that the whole of the Greek pantheon of gods had been marked by a dualism between dark and light, offering Poseidon, Hades and Dionysus as "three candidates for the role of Brunet," and observing that "no one of classical Greek times could think of Apollo as other than 'golden-haired' or blond" (Usener, 303). This simplistic view is similar, both in ease of application and in lack of further definitive context, to the allegation that identities such as "dark" and "fair" were once actually representative of the participants in a seasonal, year-cycle combat ritual. If we can accept Webster's contention that "there can really be no doubt that Dr. Farnell has correctly interpreted the Melanaigis story in itself" (Pickard-Cambridge, 120), we can accept any amount of preposterous fiction passing as scholarship.

Of far more interest is the vegetation theory view that certain of the myths concerning Dionysus were based on rituals of human sacrifice. It has often been said that the myth that prefigured Euripides' *Bacchae* was based on such a ritual. A. G. Bather's "The Problem of the *Bacchae*" of 1894 antedated the Harrison-Murray view of the ritual origins of tragedy by eighteen years and has continued to sustain interest. Bather proposed that the various stages of a ceremony from which the *Bacchae* derived could be reconstructed from folk customs illustrating the following stages: (1) the dressing up of a constructed figure as a woman; (2) leading it through the town so that all could see it; (3) setting it on a tree; (4) pelting it with sticks and stones; (5) tearing the figure to pieces and scrambling for the parts; (6) carrying the head of the figure back at racing pace; (7) attaching the head to the house. This pattern was thought to prefigure the death of Pentheus. Not all of these stages could be successfully illustrated, but several of the parallels are of interest.

Most significant, because of their diffusion and unusual character, are folk customs from Estonia, Austria, Russia, and elsewhere in which a tree is dressed like a woman, as Pentheus was, or a figure is carried affixed to a long pole, then suspended on a tree or torn apart. The folk customs seemed to Bather to be survivals of a ritual of human sacrifice, just as Frazer said of the fate of Pentheus that "the description suggests that the human victim was tied or hung to a pine-tree before being torn to pieces" (Dodds, 209).

The manner of his death links the dismemberment of Pentheus with the dismemberment of Zagreus, the Orphic version of Dionysus. A common view of both myths then is that they were based on a ritual that associated rending of a victim (*sparagmos*) with cannibalism (*omophagia*). Zagreus was the infant Dionysus. He was given certain toys to play with by the Titans who then whitened their faces with gypsum and attacked him while his attention was occupied. In order to escape them, the myth said, Zagreus went through a series of changes of shape, finally becoming a bull, in which form he was slain. The Titans dismembered Zagreus, cooked him in a cauldron, and ate him. For this they were destroyed, and the race of man was created from their ashes, while Zagreus-Dionysus was born again from his heart, which had been saved (Cook, II, 1029f.). The whitening of the faces, and perhaps even the toys, suggest a ritual. It has been thought that it was similar to that which had prefigured the *Bacchae*. George Thomson, for example, wrote that:

It cannot, of course, be doubted that behind the myth of Pentheus there lies a real death. The totemic sacrament of the primitive clan has been transformed from a simple act of magical communion into the bloody sacrifice of a secret society. Pentheus was torn to pieces by the Bacchantes as an embodiment of Dionysus, who was torn to pieces by the Titans; or, rather, the death of Dionysus was a mythical projection of the actual death reflected in the myth of Pentheus. In the myth of Dionysus, the death is followed by a resurrection; but in the ritual itself, after the substitution of a human victim, this element was necessarily eliminated, except in so far as the victim's death conferred newness of life on all in contact with his flesh and blood.   (Thomson, 131–32)

As we have noted, reconstructions of totemistic human sacrifice by vegetation theorists invariably suggest Christian communion. Farnell, speculating on the Thracian origins of Dionysianism, used the same, standard vocabulary.

. . . we may suppose that the incarnation was more often an animal or an effigy . . . devoured sacramentally by the Thracian votary, so that he or she might enjoy communion with the divinity by drinking divine blood and eating the flesh on which his spirit resided. At times of great religious exaltation or public excitement they may have eaten the priest himself in this solemn way.
                    (Farnell, V, 106)

There is no need to argue the invalidity of this view in regard to actual totemic practices. In the two myths and the folk customs we have a pattern and conjunction of symbols, the dressing in women's clothes, the dismemberment, and the tree, which clearly show shamanistic antecedents. The centrality of the tree in Dionysian concepts is shown by the fact that the god was worshiped throughout Greece as a "tree-Dionysus," as a "god of the tree," or as "the Power in the tree." The myths show that the tree associated with Dionysus was the tree as "vertical axis" in shamanist ritual, the source of the shaman's "power."

The two following facts are of primary significance in regard to the association of Dionysus both with insanity and with the tree, and in regard to the dismemberment of Pentheus that was associated with the tree: (1) The shaman is driven mad by the spirits of his ancestors who live in the tree, and recovers some degree of sanity only by shamanizing. (2) In the course of the "initiation" that transforms insanity into shamanic practice, the person undergoing the experience is taken to the sky-world or to the underworld, dismembered by the spirits, often cooked in a pot or oven, eaten by them, and then "resurrected" as a shaman. As Eliade emphasizes, *"It is only this initiatory death and resurrection that consecrates a shaman"* (Eliade, 76).

During the insanity, the period of "initiation," which often lasts several years, the person afflicted frequently acts out in a compulsive fashion the ritual, imaginary ascent that is characteristic of the shaman's trance. In Sumatra, for example, the candidate undergoing the nervous breakdown often disappears from the village, and, if he does not return,

> . . . a search is made for him and he is usually found in the top of a tree, conversing with spirits. He seems to have lost his mind, and sacrifices must be offered to restore him to sanity.
>
> (Eliade, 140)

Much the same thing occurs among the Yakut, where insanity and the initiation are thought of as dismemberment by spirits.

> Before men become shamans they are ill for a long time. They grow thin, are nothing but skin and bone. They go out of their minds, talk meaningless nonsense, keep on climbing up into the tops of larch trees. All the time they talk rubbish, as though their eyes were being put out, their bodies being cut up, as though they were being taken to pieces and eaten, as though new blood were being poured into them and so on.
>
> (Lommel, 59)

The death of Pentheus by placement on the tree and dismemberment was not intended as an image of death at all, or at least did not derive from actual death, having been prefigured by the initiatory "death and dismemberment" of shamanism. As noted, Dionysus appears again and again in mythology as a force or supernatural power that drives persons insane. We have a direct association in this context of Dionysus as "the Power in the tree," and as "render of men," "hunter of men," "the raging one," and "the mad one" (Otto, 109ff.).

The myths of Attis and Kybele show the shamanistic origins of Dionysianism. When the maenads in the *Bacchae* "raise the old, old hymn to Dionysus," Dionysianism is associated with "they who keep the rite of Cybele the Mother," and the god is spoken of as being brought "home" from Phrygia. Cybele (or Kybele) was associated, as a cult partner, with the worship of Attis in Phrygia (Syria). It seems most probable that Dionysianism had its origins there in archaic times, and the worship of Kybele-Attis was later encompassed by the worship of Zeus. The various folk customs that Bather felt had prefigured the *Bacchae* are, in fact, more or less identical with a custom associated with the worship of Attis in Roman times. There was a ritual in which a pine tree was cut down in the woods, decorated with ribbons and flowers, and brought to the sanctuary of Kybele. This tree was identified with Attis, specifically as the tree beneath which he had emasculated himself, and an effigy of a young man, "doubtless that of Attis himself," was fastened to the middle of the tree (Frazer, 370).

In a similar manner, young people in Bohemia cut down a small tree, fasten to it a doll dressed to look like a woman, and parade with it, collecting gifts (Frazer, 119). Russian villagers do much the same thing, dressing a young birch tree in women's clothing and decorating it with ribbons (Frazer, 117). In Silesia, a straw figure dressed in women's clothes is carried about on a long pole, then taken to a field and torn apart; and in Estonia, about A.D. 1500, a figure that might be either a man or a woman was carried about on a long pole and then finally set up in a tree in the woods (Bather, 250–51).

The fact that the figures associated with the trees in these folk customs are dressed as women is a significant point; the shaman is most often identified, at least in popular awareness, with the sex change that is a worldwide phenomenon in shamanistic culture and derives from the essential derangement or from a customary ritualization of identity. This is symbolized in the emasculation of Attis and was undoubtedly the basis for the dressing of Pentheus in women's clothes in the *Bacchae*. The two examples of figures raised high on poles identify them as representations of the shaman's ascent by means of the ritual pole as "tree." The ribbons that may decorate the trees are like those in a Buryat shaman's ritual (Eliade, 117–18).

There is good reason to believe, as Bogoras has suggested, that Kybele, the strange progenitor and cult partner of Attis, was the archetypal "mother" in shamanistic cosmology, the animal ancestor that controlled the animal souls and the souls of the clan. Kybele was also identified with Agdistis, who seems to have been an alternate identity of her (Rose, 170). Agdistis-Kybele was a bisexual being that had sprung from the ground and then had its male genitals shorn by the gods. We find in this representation the metaphysical belief in superior being as a synthesis and resolution of sexual polarity arrived at, or symbolized by, a sex change like that associated with shamanism. The severed genitals of Agdistis produced a tree that grew up from them, clearly the world-tree or vertical axis of shamanism. Attis was then born from a nymph that had been impregnated by a leaf or blossom from this tree. Kybele, however, drove Attis insane, just as shamans are driven insane by their ancestor spirits, and he then emasculated himself beneath a pine tree, again repeating the same hieratic symbolism of the shamanistic attempt at achieving neuter being.

While the *Bacchae* contained an ancient memory of "dismemberment" in shamanic initiation, the Orphic myth of Dionysus (Zagreus) used a similar schema of images for didactic purposes. Zagreus was hacked into pieces, cooked in a kettle, and eaten by the Titans, who were the "ancestors" in the sense that mankind was composed from their ashes. The Orphic movement, which appeared late in the seventh century or early sixth century B.C., drew upon previous myths for their material, but consciously, even intellectually, modified them. "All the evidence points to [Orphism] having been in its origin the product of a few individual minds active over a limited period of time" (Guthrie, 120).

Zagreus was identified with, and was meant to be, Dionysus, but this distinct name was apparently given so as not to conflict with existing tradition. The myth pictured Zagreus-Dionysus as an infant so as to make the statement that he represented the "childhood" or "early age" of Dionysianism. It was an etiological myth, and the events it portrays show clearly that the early age from which Dionysianism evolved was intended to be understood as identified with shamanism. The boiling and eating of Zagreus-Dionysus corresponds in detail with the initiation experience of the shaman.

The insanity that compels the victim to become a shaman is directly associated with distortions of the body image. These are not only delusionary beliefs that the person has been taken to the sky-world or to the underworld and is being cut up and dismembered by spirits; among the Yakut, white froth flows from the mouth of the victim and his joints trickle blood (Lommel, 56). High fever and other somatic changes accompanying the psychosis have caused the traditional images of shamanistic dismemberment to be described as baking in an oven or boiling in a cauldron.

When the souls of the dead shamanistic ancestors have instructed
the Buryat novice, whom they are forcing to become a shaman, in
heaven, they boil him so that he shall become ready (mature, prop-
erly cooked). In antiquity all shamans were boiled, so that they
should learn the shamanistic knowledge. While this is going on he
lies for seven days as though dead.   (Lommel, 56)

The myth of Zagreus-Dionysus cooked and eaten by the Titans seems
clearly to have derived from this traditional representation of shamanic
insanity and dismemberment. The whitening of their faces by the
Titans, the toys given to Zagreus, and the shape changes he goes
through when attacked place the myth in the context of ritual in
general and of the shamanistic seance in particular.

The Altai and Goldi shamans cover their faces with suet so as not to
be recognized by the spirits; that is, they use this device as a disguise,
just as the Titans did (Eliade, 166). The "toys" given to Zagreus were
the ritual instruments of the shamanistic seance. Of these, the most
significant is the mirror into which Zagreus was gazing, his attention
occupied when the Titans surprised him. The shaman uses such a mirror
in order to "see the world" and to "place the spirits"; that is, to
concentrate his attention so that he can go into trance (Eliade, 154).
The other "toys" have not been identified with any precision. An
Orphic fragment speaks of them only in vague general terms as "tops of
different sorts, and jointed dolls, and fair golden apples from the clear-
voiced Hesperides." Clement of Alexandria, writing about A.D. 200,
adds that they were actually "a knuckle-bone, a ball, tops, apples, a
mirror, a lump of wool" (Guthrie, 121). Clement's words for "tops"
seem to have been *konos* and *rhombos*, which Guthrie translates as
"pine-cone" and "bull-roarer," clearly associating them with Dionysianism. A rhomb, however, is listed among the equipment of a North
American shaman (Eliade, 178), and the objects, spoken of with intentional euphemism, were most likely not tops but similar shapes
suspended at the end of a thread for purposes of divination (Eliade,
257). They had been "brought back" from the "Hesperides" visited in
trance.

Perhaps the most significant representation in the myth of Zagreus-
Dionysus is that of the shape changing. It is a key to the meaning of
other myths in which Dionysus employs this technique to drive persons
insane, and to the *Bacchae* in which he twice appears to Pentheus as

transformed into a bull. According to Cook's account, which includes the Orphic fragments, Zagreus-Dionysus became a young Zeus, an ancient Kronos, a baby, a young man, a lion, a horse, a horned snake, a tiger, and then finally a bull, in which form he was slain (Cook, II, 1029f.). In the seance, mesmerization induced by the songs, drumming, and acts of magic causes the shaman's series of transformations to become apparent reality.

> . . . this strange figure, with its wild and frenzied appearance, its ventriloquistic cries and its unearthly falsetto gabble . . . is no longer a human being, but the thing it personifies. . . . If the shaman ejaculates that he is . . . a bear, forthwith it is a bear that they behold . . . if he says that the dance-house is full of spirits they will see them in every corner.   (Charles, 119)

The moment of death in the myth is a dramatic one. As Zagreus-Dionysus, in his transformations, arrived at the form of a bull, "A bellowing in mid-air from the throat of Hera was the signal for his fate" (Cook, II, 1029). This striking image seems to have been suggested by the ventriloquism of the shaman that projected sounds and voices so that they were heard to originate in space.

Among the Yakut, the bull was the supreme shamanic identity.

> The music swells and rises to the highest pitch . . . Then sombrely the voice of the shaman chants the following obscure fragments:
> Mighty bull of the earth . . . Horse of the steppes!
> I, the mighty bull, bellow!
> I, the horse of the steppes, neigh!
> I, the man set above all other beings!
>   (Lommel, 69)

The shaman's identification with the bull and with the horse, the vehicle in trance flight, is understood as the manifestation of an animal soul that has made the shaman supernatural, unique, and thus set apart from others in society. The association of Dionysus with the bull and other animals is derived from a similar world view, and his transformations in mythology are particularly significant. Dionysus in *Bacchae* appears twice to Pentheus as a bull (618f., 920f.). The key to this image is that he so *appears* and that he has (or has not) changed from what he was. These are episodes of delusion in which the world or persons appear to have changed. When Dionysus drove the daughters of Minyas insane, he did so by appearing to them in he form of a young girl and then suddenly transformed himself into a bull, a lion, and then a panther (Otto, 110). The schema of this shape changing, as a technique, motif, or standardized image in myth, derived from the shamanistic seance but was used to refer directly to insanity as such, the "change of world" experienced in its occurrence.

The myth of Pentheus on which *Bacchae* is based is one of four in which we can perceive a similar pattern of adaptation from shamanism. They pertain to four different cities and present, as E. R. Dodds says, "an odd fixity of outline": (1) The myth from Orchomenus tells of the three daughters of the king, Minyas, who became insane, were taken with a craving for human flesh, and chose by lots the child of one of them to be torn to pieces and eaten. (2) The myth from Argos tells of the three daughters of King Proetus who went mad, induced the women of the city to kill their children and eat them and to go as bacchantcs to the mountains. (3) The myth from Thebes tells of the three daughters of King Cadmus who were driven mad by Dionysus, made to lead the women of the city as bacchantes to the mountains, and destroyed the son of one of them, the king, Pentheus. (4) The myth from Eleutherae tells of the three daughters of the king, Eleuther, who were driven insane for refusing to worship Dionysus when the god appeared to them in a "vision."

Dodds writes:

> . . . always it is the king's daughters who go mad; always there are three of them (corresponding to the three *thiasoi* of maenads which existed at Thebes and elsewhere in historical times); regularly they murder their children, or the child of one of them.
>
> (Dodds [B], xxvi)

Dodds suggests that these were historical events, murders of children by royalty, that had been given a triadic structure by ritual. "History no doubt repeats itself, but it is only ritual that repeats itself exactly" (Dodds [B], xxvii). But there is no reason to suppose that these myths relate to history at all or that they reveal the nature of actual events. The pattern of the king with three daughters is a convention of structure that can be inherent in myth itself, and the myth can pertain neither to history nor to ritual.

Plutarch records that triadic allusions in common speech were conventional references to greater numbers, to multiplicity. He observed that "we have a habit" of using triadic expressions to mean a great many, as in using "thrice" in the expression "thrice happy" to mean "many times" (*Isis and Osiris*, 89). The three daughters in the myth pattern then signify "many daughters." The myths themselves indicate why the king, by means of this symbolic expression, was said to have many daughters. The "king's three daughters" linked the mythologized royal house with the women of the city, who were his "many daughters."

The people of Orchomenus, for example, spoke of the Oleiae ("Murderesses") as the women descended from the family of Minyas; that is, as the "daughters" who figured in the myth. This must certainly have been a figurative allusion, not a literal truth. In two other of the myths, the three daughters of the kings of Argos and Thebes lead all the women of their cities to the mountains to become bacchantes, again identifying the "three" with the "many."

In this pattern, the city as an entity identified with royal personifications seems to have developed from the shamanistic clan pattern in which all were members of a group identified with important ancestor souls or spirits. If we begin with the correlation between the myths of Zagreus-Dionysus and Pentheus as based upon shamanistic "dismembering," the key to the grouping of the four very similar myths becomes apparent. The children destroyed by the women are like the shaman driven mad and dismembered by the ancestor spirits, the souls of the clan. These souls are conceived of in a generalized way as feminine and as created by a mother-beast, all living at the base of the clan tree (Anisimov [S], 97, [C] 168–69). This would seem to be a reasonable source for the transposition onto the women in the myths, as the "mother-beasts" who eat their children, of the *sparagmos* and *omophagia* of the shamanistic initiatory insanity.

The myth of the daughters of Minyas, who choose a child by lot, seems to be saying that insanity will make its "selections" by the methods of chance. In general, one judgment made by the myths is that the women who turn to maenadism "kill" or "sacrifice" their children by involvement with a mode that has no concern with the bearing and rearing of children, thus breaking off the lineal descent of the clan (the city as symbolic entity) and sacrificing the future of the line. The murder of children, in these purely symbolic terms, means the sacrifice of the future both as individual experience, to madness, and as perpetuity of the "family" in time. The myths from Argos and from Orchomenus relate that the madness was cured by Dionysian priests or dances (Thomson, 136). But we may be reasonably sure that no ritual murder of children by insane daughters of kings gave symbolic configuration to the myths of Dionysianism in the four cities represented. Behind the myth of Pentheus lay not a "ghastly ritual in which a man is torn to pieces" (Otto, 109) and eaten as a human sacrifice, but another ritual, with its own horror, in which the mind was lost.

The "apparitions" of Dionysus to those he drives insane relate indirectly to the practices of shamanistic illusionism that characterized the cult of Dionysus. In the festivals of Dionysus, miraculous streams of wine gushed forth in phenomena that must have been based on mass delusion. In Elis, a carefully sealed room containing three empty basins was opened the next day to show them filled with wine (Otto, 97). The trick is similar to that of a Chinese "doctor" leaving a sword in a sealed room and next day showing there the blood of the specters it had slain (de Groot, 993); both probably used secret entrances to the sealed room. Chinese pseudo-shamanism also practiced changing water into wine (van Gulik, 149). Walter Otto cites a fragment of Sophocles that spoke of so-called one-day vines and refers to another example of the miraculous growth of plants.

> Euphorion knew of a festival of Dionysus in Achaean Aigai in which the sacred vines bloomed and ripened during the cult dances of the chorus so that already by evening considerable quantities of wine could be pressed.   (Otto, 99)

In a similar manner, Chinese magicians "planted dates and melons and after a few moments one could eat their ripe fruit" (van Gulik, 120). If the Eleusinian mysteries did show grain that ripened magically like this, the trick was also those of North American shamans who "are credited with the power to make a grain of wheat germinate and sprout before the eyes of the audience" (Eliade, 315). Something like this appears to have been practiced in the Liknophoria festival and in secret Orphic initiations for Dionysus Liknites, centering on use of the *liknon*, a shovel-shaped winnowing fan. Illustrations show the initiate masked with a cloth (Harrison [P], 519–20), and there is a striking parallel with Munda shaman initiation in India, in which the initiate in trance stirs rice in a winnowing fan and both he and the *guru* are covered with a cloth (Rahmann, 684).

With this awareness of the shamanistic basis of Dionysianism, the origins of the satyr play and of old comedy can be reconstructed. Both evolved from trance dances in which animal costume, or thereomorphic identity, signifies the nature of trance possession. There has been reason enough for the confusion that has designated the satyrs as "a wild and gross cult" (Ridgeway [O], 15), as representations of an alien people, the Satrai (Harrison [P], 379), or as personifications of "spirits of the wild life of woods and hills" (Rose, 156). Even as shown in pottery designs engaged in cult activities, satyrs are often already mythologized, not shown realistically, being pictured with pointed ears, horses' tails that grow directly from their bodies, and sometimes horses' hooves instead of feet. The merger of man with horse most probably derives from identification with the horse ridden on the shaman's trance flight and with the spiritual horse-identity assumed by the shaman. The Buryat or Muria shaman appears to represent trance flight, as well as practice it, by riding a "horse stave," a rod decorated with the carved head of a horse. But there is an even more fundamental meaning of the horse-rider relationship as based on the nature and dynamics of the trance state as such. In the dissociation of consciousness, the body becomes a "horse" for the possessing god as "rider." In voodoo prac-tices, the trancers are known as the "horses" of the *loa*, the gods who seize and "mount" them (Métraux, 24). Trancers of the *bori* spirits of the Hausas of West and North Africa are similar, "a male being a *doki* (horse), and a woman a *godiya* (mare) because the bori mount their heads or upon the backs of their necks, and ride them" (Tremearne, 275). In North Thailand, "mediums are called *maa khii*, that is, 'horses ridden' by spirits" (Tambiah, 283). Likewise, "the Greek oracle at Delphi was mounted by the God Apollo who rode on the nape of her neck" (Lewis, 58).

The horse-man satyrs represent a complete merger of the horse-rider configuration. But they are very like another trance dance merger of horse and rider into a single image, commonly known as the "hobby horse," in which the trancer wears about his body a framework repre-sentation of a horse or rides upon such a representation. In Bali, as observed by Jane Belo, the hobby horse that is ridden is made of rattan with a head and tail of leaves or fibers.

The player would start out riding the hobby horse, being so to speak, the horseman. But in his trance activity he would soon clearly become identified with the horse—he would prance, gallop about, stamp and kick as a horse—or perhaps it would be fairer to

say that he would be horse and rider in one. For though he would
sit on the hobby horse, his legs would serve from the beginning as
the legs of the beast.   (Belo [T], 213)

There are many survivals of such hobby-horse dances in the folk
performances of Europe, and evidence for them can be found from
virtually all over the world, in diverse and unrelated cultures.

And now there is no end to it. We are drawn from dance to dance,
from country to country, from the Basque *Zamalzain* and the Ger-
man *Schimmelreitermaske* (mask of the man on the white horse) to
the ecstatic hobby-horse dance of the Javanese. . . . From ancient
China in the north comes another horse dance, the characteristics of
which are not known. . . . Is not the dance of Mallorca that same
hobby-horse dance which is performed to the point of extreme
ecstasy by the Rumanians and Bulgarians. . . ?   (Sachs, 338)

The type of representation is not known, but in the ecstatic dances of
the Himalayas in honor of the god Airi, the truly possessed are called
the god's "slaves" or "horses" (Wood, 44). The rider-horse relationship
is everywhere that of god-trancer or consciousness-body. Again, this is
shown by the description of trance mediums as observed by Verrier
Elwin in India.

At Metawand I watched for several hours the antics of a medium
who was carrying on his shoulders the wooden horse of his clan god
and at Bandopal a medium carrying an imaginary horse on his
shoulders "ambled, caracoled, pranced and plunged" for two miles
before my slow-moving car as we made our way into the jungle. . . .
"The god rides upon him," they told me, "and he cannot stop
dancing for days at a time."   (Elwin, 21)

It makes no difference that these trancers both *carry* their horses
rather than riding them or that one horse is invisible. The reversed
relationship between horse and rider indicates the *burden* of trance
possession, just as does the god who "rides" the medium. It is this
relationship which shows the chorus of Greek old comedy to have
evolved from thereomorphic trance possession. It is generally agreed
that old comedy was based on the parabasis of a thereomorphic chorus,
representing and enacting animal identities, such as those illustrated on

certain pieces of pottery. Theories differ concerning the form of the parabasis (Sifakis, 16–17), but it may be defined in general terms as the entrance dance song, presentation, and exit dance song of the chorus. At any rate, the importance of these choruses seems established. "In the whole prehistory of drama there is perhaps no other point of more general agreement than the importance of the thereomorphic choruses (i.e. choruses of men dressed up as animals, or riding on animals), represented on Attic vases of the sixth and early fifth century, as evidence for the origins of comedy" (Sifakis, 3).

One vase, thought to represent or prefigure the chorus in Aris- tophanes' *Knights*, shows men wearing masks mounted on other men who represent horses dancing upright, hands on their knees. The "horses" have tails and their faces look out from beneath horse-head masks worn on top of the head. At least three vases show helmeted riders on dolphins, and two of these (perhaps the third) picture the flute player who clearly shows them to be dance choruses. This is significant, because the artist in each case has rather curiously chosen to show the riders seated upon actual dolphins, rather than upon per- formers costumed as dolphins. In a similar manner, another vase pic- tures a chorus seated upon huge ostriches, rather than upon humans costumed as ostriches. Granting the degree of artistic license evidenced in Greek art, the representation of actual animals as "vehicles" for the chorus is most probably based on the heightened identification of the performers with such animals in trance. That which shows the "horses" as disguised humans would be an enactment of the basic trance rider- horse relationship. Mythology tells how Dionysus transformed the pirates who had captured him into dolphins. Essentially, this image represents the complete metamorphosis of consciousness that occurs when persons become insane, but it may have been suggested by a common type of Dionysian trance performance in which the transfor- mation was only temporary. Arion was said to have traveled to Tainaron on the back of a dolphin, which was probably legend's way of saying that he brought there a "supernatural" possession-dithyramb of this type.

Other choruses in old comedy seem not to have used persons mounted on dancers, although the choruses were still thereomorphic, representing a given type of animal. As versions of *Birds* by Aris- tophanes, Crates, and Magnes suggest, this representation was popular. It is pictured in a pottery design which shows a chorus of men with beards wearing winglike constructions fastened to their arms and with

14. Attic black-figured skyphos showing youths riding dolphins.

15. Another view of the same design, showing youths riding ostriches and a flute player.

feathered bodies. A flute player and vines in the background show them to be Dionysiac dancers. The image of bird flight relates them to dances of the maenads, who are so often depicted on vases precisely as Lawler has said, "having their hands twisted into their garments in such a way as to suggest birds' wings when their hands are lifted" (Lawler, 76). Euripides' *Bacchae* (748) describes how the maenads who had run mad flew like birds across the fields. The three daughters of Minyas, driven mad by Dionysus, ran the fields in this way until Hermes changed them into birds. Pindar commented with wonder upon Arion's creation of the choral dithyramb:

> Whence were revealed the new charms of Dionysus, with the accompaniment of the ox-driving dithyramb? Who made new means of guidance in the harness of steeds, or set the twin king of birds on the temples of the gods?   (Ridgeway [O], 5)

The reference seems to be to the new dithyramb as artistic control of the satyrs as trance horses and perhaps of the maenads as "birds." The bird-identity relates not only to flight but to trance flight, and this concept and costume are among the oldest associated with shamanism. Weston La Barre relates drawings found at Lascaux and other prehistoric sites to other evidence of this symbolism.

> Thus, however variously interpreted, the majority of students would agree that the bird-headed man with the bird staff is a bird shaman, perhaps like the bird-headed men at the Roc de Sers cognate with the bison-masked shamans, the chamois shamans, the dancing shaman of Trois Frères, etc. Not only ancient context but also contemporary ethnology support this view. According to the recent Levin-Potapov anthology on Siberia, the Altai and Kachin shaman's garb symbolizes a bird, and birds are associated with shamanic spirit travels.   (La Barre, 419)

The shaman's costume has fringes in back and hanging from the arms, representing feathers and wings. "The Mongolian shaman has wings on his shoulders and feels himself changing into a bird on donning his costume. A Tungus shaman declared, 'A bird costume is necessary for flight into another world' " (Lindsay, 248).

The animal choruses are most usually taken to be thereomorphic demons (Sifakis, 79). This doesn't mean much, since any kind of Greek demons would be so ancient that nothing is known about them. The primordial type of shamanistic animal dance would be that of a hunting culture in which the dancers represented the animal spirits, the "boss spirits" of animal species, with whom the shaman could establish contact, as among the Bacairi of western Brazil. Among tribes in Bolivia, these same spirits are demons, hostile to mankind (Zerries, 266). The "demon" hypothesis, of which there is actually no suggestion in the choruses, is an aspect of other "totemic" interpretations, but the choruses are apparently late developments, so speculation in regard to their origin is difficult. However, a comparison with similar forms found elsewhere can be useful.

If we consider the choruses represented by the titles of such plays as *Gall-Flies, Ants, Wasps*, and *Bees*, we might feel that thereomorphic enactment in general, and particularly that based on trance possession, would be impossible or unlikely. Reich felt that primitive peoples didn't have dances such as these, and that even as a solo a fish or ant dance would be unthinkable (Sifakis, 83). In principle, this is incorrect. It is the unusual nature of the dancer's identification, not the difficulty in representation, that suggests that these are trance dances. Possession dances of the Tonga of Zambia include animals, such as the elephant, jackal, and crane, but also possession by the spirits of modern vehicles, such as the train, motor boat, and airplane (Colson, 86–87). In Bali, *sanghyang* trance enactments include the white horse, toad, snake, and turtle, but also objects, such as the broom and the potlid. The potlid trancer has bells and the potlid tied to his hand, and he goes about striking things rhythmically. The broom trancer has a small broom tied to his hand and sweeps in small circles (Belo [T], 201). These enactments and dances suggest that the choruses of *Wasps, Frogs*, and even *Clouds* could have developed from trance dances within the Dionysian cult. Innovation was certainly a factor in regard to the choruses of old comedy, as it has been in the introduction of new types of possession in the Tonga dances. The *sanghyang* performers are insulted for comic purposes, and there is much playfulness connected with them. The festival background of the thereomorphic choruses would seem to have much in common with African masquerades, where much comedy is associated with masked trance performances. It is said that a chorus of stilt walkers shown on an Attic vase may "anticipate a chorus of Attic comedy" (Trendall and Webster, 21), and stilt walkers identified with possession by water spirits dance in African masquerades.

The hypothesis of an origin in trance enactment would also seem to explain another type of old comedy chorus which otherwise seems quite bizarre and inexplicable. Titles such as *Dionysoi* and *Odysses*, which are plurals of proper names, must have had choruses which multiplied individual identity into choruses of Dionysuses and Odyseuses (Sifakis, 90). Multiple possession by a single identity, which can result in comic encounters, could have suggested this type of chorus.

It seems most probable that the thereomorphic chorus that served as the basis for old comedy did not derive from ancient animal dances, but rather that it was an epiphenomenon suggested by the more serious trance involvement of the basic Dionysian trance dance complex. The thereomorphic chorus is often thought of as the *komus*, from which he word "comedy" comes, but the actual origin and meaning of the word are unknown, and it may not be of Attic origin. Philology is not a game, but the following correspondences in shamanistic cultures are of interest in this context. "The Soiot call [the jews' harp] *komus* (the Yakut, *homus* or *hamys*), but the Altaians (using the term in the narrowest sense), who also have the word *komus*, use it to designate the stringed instrument resembling the Russian *balalaika*, which only shamans play" (Czaplicka, 216).

The satyrs, as shown in vase paintings, have three distinct identities: (1) they are trance horses practicing cathartic and shamanistic ritual; (2) they are performers in comic situations, dances, and dramas; (3) they appear in scenes from historical mythology which represent in symbolic terms the shamanistic origins of Dionysianism. From the relationship between these three distinct identities, and from the reasons for them, we can reconstruct the origins of the satyr play. For the satyrs were neither originally nor essentially creatures of comedy and satire. We forget this because, misrepresented by others, they came to misrepresent themselves. But Pollux's account of their dances on Malea leaves us a single vivid image: "There were Silens and with them satyrs dancing in terror" (Pickard-Cambridge, 116). And we know that these were the "raving satyrs" who had stolen the "primal drum" of the trance dance from the Korybantes and Kuretes. Caricature and suppression of the satyrs, the traditional followers of Dionysus, was due to their identification with shamanistic origins and to their association with dithyrambic music and with an archaic, ritual phallicism.

Two pictures on a bowl dating from the mid-sixth century B.C. show a "fat man" and a satyr each riding a platform conveyed by numerous bearers and supporting a huge phallus pole that they seem to "ride" (Pickard-Cambridge, Plate 15). In the background of each are the vines

16. Processional wagon of Dionysus, an animal-ship, with the god holding the characteristic vines that symbolize intoxication and accompanied by two satyrs playing pipes.

17. Phallus pole with animal head carried by bearers and ridden by a hairy satyr.

18. A similar phallus pole ridden by a fat-man, with the characteristic vines of intoxication in background.

of Dionysus that symbolize the trance. Each of the phallus poles has a prominent eye at the end, with other eyelike designs down the shaft. One of the poles also has what appear to be animal ears rising above the eye. A basic function of representations of the phallus in the ancient world was to ward off the "evil eye," but the eye of the phallus pole reminds one of the eye on the prow of seagoing vessels, which might have been apotropaic but was also a "seeing" or "opening of the way"; and this association, coupled with the horselike ears on the pole, indicates that the poles were vehicles of the trance flight.

The phallus poles are set at an angle of about forty-five degrees and appear to have derived from a tradition of somewhat similar poles in shamanistic culture. The well-known horse sacrifice of the Altai, for example, suspends the dead horse on a pole set at just this angle. It is run through the horse from the rear so that it points it upward at an angle, aimed, as it were, toward the place where its soul will go, and the function of the shaman in the ceremony is to accompany the soul there in trance flight. The *obo* poles characteristic of Siberia are also angled in this way and seem to have served a similar function; they are erected at the sites of past disasters and seem to have served to point the direction of flight the soul has taken (Diozegi, 327). These are variants of the shamanic tree as the vertical axis of trance flight. A fragment which shows satyrs riding on a ship carried by "komasts" (Pickard-Cambridge, Fig. 4) probably represents an enactment of trance flight. It would then have been similar to that of the Salish Indians in which "the journey to the underworld in a boat is made graphically visible to the onlookers by a crew of ten shamans in rows of four carrying out paddling movements in front of the community, while the chief shaman plays the part of steersman. . . . Spirits that fall upon him during his journey are played by boys carrying torches" (Lommel, 137–38).

It can be shown that Dionysian ritual phallicism, like the processional phallus poles, was directly associated with trance flight. It has been thought, of course, that Dionysian phallicism relates to vegetation magic. Frazer proposed, on the basis of a few scattered examples, that the copulation of married couples, representing the order of nature, was a primitive, archetypal method of inducing the growth of vegetation with sympathetic magic by miming in this way the "marriage of trees and plants." The apparent anarchic lasciviousness of the satyrs could not have been a representation of this necessary order. The tribes of the northwest Amazon associate the fertility of the fields with male potency and perform a masked dance in which males masturbate large

19. Ecstatic maenads with tambourines, thyrsi, torches and libations before a Dionysus column or post.

phalluses and then carry and scatter the invisible semen everywhere for magical purposes (Zerries, 280). There would seem to be a possible analogy here with Dionysian practices, but the fact is that the association of fertility magic with Dionysian phallicism has been a theoretical attribution incorrectly arrived at, as can be seen when the basic evidence is considered.

In many pottery designs, satyrs appear either completely naked or with their genitals exposed by brief trunks to which the horsetail is attached. The renderings are often very realistic, and the trunks seem to represent the costume in satyr plays and dances. Several of these designs show the satyr's penis erect and/or thrown about by the movement of the dance (Pickard-Cambridge [F], Figs. 38–40, 49). The trunks emphasize the phallicism, but nudity in performance was not exceptional. Pyrrhic dancers at the Panathenaia "were naked save for a light helmet and a shield on the left arm" (Lindsay, 107), and by rough count seventy-five of the one hundred and five pottery designs purported to illustrate the performances of tragedy in the Trendall and Webster volume show some or all naked figures, though these are sometimes women, which would be impossible, and much must be due to artistic license. At any rate, the phallicism of the satyrs, not to be confused with the use of an artificial phallus in old comedy and in mimes, derives from the phallic Dionysus.

Dionysus in ritual was characteristically worshiped in the form of a post or column running from floor to ceiling, costumed, with a mask representing his face, and from which branches often sprang. Maenads and satyrs dance and make offerings to this image. As noted, it is Dionysus as the the shamanistic vertical axis. Related to this is a statue-like post, apparently often life-sized, topped by the bearded head of Dionysus and with an erect phallus (Trendall and Webster, 26–27). This is known as a herm because similar phallic posts have been identified as associated with Hermes. One picture shows in the foreground a Dionysus herm with an erect phallus, while in the background are the sillhouettes of another such phallic pedestal-with-bust and of a dancing satyr, crouched, also with an erection (Goldman).

Analysis of the mythological symbolism of Dionysus and Hermes shows that both gods were identified with shamanic trance flight represented in terms of the copulation of two snakes and strongly suggests that the phallicism of the herms, and hence of the satyrs, derives from this source. Orphic myth tells us that Zagreus-Dionysus was born from the union of Zeus and his own daughter (Persephone or Kore) when they copulated in the form of snakes. The daughter had been born when Zeus copulated with his own mother (Rhea or Demeter) when both were in the form of snakes. The daughter, mother of Dionysus, had horns and four eyes, two located in the normal position and two in her forehead, and also had another face on the back of her head. I take this to be an "iconization" of shamanic shape changing which Orphism did not find overly attractive, and which figures also in the death of Zagreus-Dionysus. The symbolism of the *caduceus* staff of Hermes, with two snakes twined into the so-called Heraclean knot, derives from the intercourse in the form of snakes told of in this myth (Cook, I, 398). Hermes, a very ancient god, as conductor of souls and as a messenger between gods and men, is very clearly a personification and deification of the shamanic function. The shaman often wore wings on his hat, just as Hermes did (Eliade, 155,157). The caduceus staff is again the vertical axis of trance flight. "The prime function of the caduceus is to be the instrument of Hermes as conductor of souls. In Homer it puts men to sleep, a property which makes Raingeard ask whether behind this tradition of its qualities lies an association with hypnotism or cataleptic trance" (Butterworth, 154). The snakes on the caduceus are schematized into an abstraction that is like a figure eight open at the top, probably to suggest the world of reality that opens into the world of the gods in the trance flight.

The association of the copulation of snakes with trance flight is found in a very ancient level or stratum of shamanism The copulation is represented in the Naga (snake) worship of South India (Devi, 129), and detailed information derives from Australia. There, the shaman lying in trance dreams of flying and "the shaman's power 'rises' in his body and causes his penis to become erect." The soul of the shaman then rides on a snake that thus rises, but remains linked to his body by a thin thread that comes from the penis or navel.

Before the beginning of a dream-flight the dreamer has the feeling that he is climbing a tree, from which he rises up into the air. Often the shaman—in his dream—has to lean a woman against the trunk of this tree and climb over her up the tree. In the air, during the flight, the shaman rides on a snake. Often he copulates with this snake during the flight. Often, too he believes that he is lying between two snakes which copulate during the flight.   (Lommel, 99)

Zagreus-Dionysus was "born" of such copulation, and it is represented as the instrument of Hermes' travels. This leads to a logical conclusion similar to that which has been arrived at on the basis of other evidence. "The Caduceus-god was, therefore, the predecessor of the Priapic herm-god. The two-sex snakes conveyed the same idea as the phallus" (Frothingham, 211). Scholarship has already disentangled Hermes from vegetation theory. Jacqueline Chittenden has observed that "the views are all inconclusive," but "Hermes has almost nothing to do with the fertility of the earth." Norman Brown in four brilliant pages does the same. "Phallic symbols of the cult of Hermes were placed on mountaintops, rural waysides, state boundaries, city streets, in the doorways and courtyards of houses, in gymnasia and libraries, in sacred precincts, and on graves; which of these is an appropriate place for a fertility symbol?" (Brown, 35–36). These are the herms with which Dionysus was also identified. Their use is clearly apotropaic, and they almost certainly derive from the small wooden figures called *darisal, terke*, and *daragun* in Siberian shamanism that are posted to guard the actual as well as the mythological boundaries of the clan and the "road" of the shaman's tree.

The copulation of snakes as trance flight is one element in an interlocking pattern of shamanistic symbolism that allows interpretation of other myths associated with Dionysianism. The Thraco-Phrygian god Sabazios, "a sort of savage un-Hellenized Dionysus" (Dodds, 194), is associated with the worship of Attis (Cook, I, 399). Copulations with mother and daughter, as in the myth of Zagreus-Dionysus, are done in the form of snakes and then of bulls. The second is achieved only after Sabazios shows the genitals of a newly gelded ram, pretending they are his own. The reference, as in the cult of Attis, is to the sex change of the shaman, and intercourse can still be accomplished in trance flight. A relief from the Roman period shows Sabazios surrounded by the shamanistic symbols (Cook, I, 392–93). His foot is on a ram's head, the symbol of his castration, and in his right hand he holds a pine cone, such as topped the thyrsus staff of the maenads. A snake twines upward around a post, the vertical axis, on which a bird is perched, symbol of the trance flight, and from which a tree grows, rather as if it grows from the bird. Next to the bird-tree-post is a caduceus. Flanking the head of Sabazios, between his own and the heads of the women that figure in the myth-copulations, are what appear to be head-sized eyeless masks with horns. The shaman is often blindfolded or wears an eyeless mask to concentrate on inner vision. Initiates in the rites for Sabazios were reported to have participated in a practice of "passing a golden adder through their bosoms and out below" (Cook, I, 394), apparently identifying the snake with the soul and with the penis and miming its trance flight.

The coupling snakes of trance flight also provide the key to the myths of Teiresias and Melampus, figures associated with Dionysianism. Teiresias was blinded, obtaining inner vision, and turned into a woman, again the shamanic sex change, when he saw two snakes coupling and killed the female. Melampus was a famous seer who gained his powers when his servants killed two snakes they saw coupling, but he burned the bodies, cared for the young, and they licked his ears so that he could understand the speech of all creatures. It was he who then cured the daughters of Proëtus and the women of Argos of their insanity by means of Dionysian cathartic dances. His myth suggests that he had been given the healing power of a shamanism that had been "killed" by the culture. In both cases the myths symbolize a manner of gaining the power of a "seer" which is essentially identical with that of the Australian shaman.

> The soul of the man who is becoming a shaman leaves him. His body lies asleep. It is a deep sleep and no one dares to wake the sleeper, even if this sleep lasts for days. During the sleep the soul goes to the water-hole from which it originally came. It does not remain in this water-hole, however, but dives down from there into the innermost part of the earth. There, after a long journey through dark water, it suddenly comes to a brightly lit cave in which two snakes, a male and a female, are mating. From the union of these two snakes there continually spring "child seeds"—many of which enter into the shaman's soul, so that henceforth he bears more soul-strength than an ordinary person.   (Lommel, 50–51).

Asclepius, the god of healing who received his power from a centaur, Chiron, would "actually" seem to have received it in this way. He is identified with a single snake climbing a tree or up his polelike staff, and he was the son of the mantic Apollo. To this we may add the myth of the fate of Cadmus and Harmonia, described in the *Bacchae*, who are transformed into a pair of snakes for defiance of Dionysus. Cadmus and Harmonia are transformed back into the animal ancestors, progenitors of the clan, sentenced to live again the archaic Dionysianism, a shamanism, that "dismembered" Pentheus. The sentence has the effect of a déjà vu. It is said that as snakes they will lead a great barbarian horde, incommensurable in numbers, that will plunder Greece and be turned back only when it has desecrated the shrine of Apollo itself (*Bacchae*, 1333ff.). Worship of Dionysus in Athens had been placed within the temple of Apollo, apparently to resolve a tension of polarized opposites, of ecstasy and logos. In a sense, Dionysianism remained a perpetual desecration of the Apollonian. In sentencing Harmonia and Cadmus to the barbarism of his own archaic origins, Dionysus draws again the rational limits of his worship, as he does throughout the drama.

The *agalma* drawn in a cart at the City Dionysia was a winged, birdlike phallus, again the identification with trance flight. One of the fragments of phalli found around the temple of Dionysus on Delos is birdlike (Sifakis [S], 7). These may be from monuments commemorating the victories of *choregoi*, so we may say that at a late date the phallus was identified with the ego. Its basic function was clearly apotropaic. The exaggerated phallus worn in mimes and in old comedy needs no other justification than comedy.

A satyr with a huge erection is shown chasing a maenad, but this is clearly a caricature (Pickard-Cambridge, IIb). It is possible that satyr rituals were licentious. Shamanistic rituals sometimes used trance for the arousal of sexual passion, as that in which the shaman as horse causes the women as mares to leap upon him in erotic ecstasy (Lommel, 74). But there is good reason to believe that this was not actually the case in regard to the satyrs as cultists. It is necessary to separate their ritual identity from that attributed to them by popular mythology. Their satyr plays represented silens and satyrs as debauched, drunken, and lascivious. But these were caricatures, just as were the characters of the gods and heroes to whom the satyr chorus devoted its satiric attention in these plays. It is probable that the popular caricature of the satyrs as drunken and licentious was as slanderous and "delusionary" as Pentheus's belief about the maenads. It can be shown that popular mythology about the satyrs subjected them to parody and satire for conceptual and didactic reasons. Made ludicrous by the society and world view in which they found themselves, the satyrs turned the weapon of the comic back upon their accusers in the satyr play. In considering how this situation came about, we may best proceed by tracing the history of the centaurs.

The most ancient man-horse or trance horse was the centaur. The earliest pictures of them show figures of men with the body and rear legs of horses appended, as if crudely attached. In time, this composite being becomes more harmonious, the body of the horse is merged more completely with the torso of a man that rises from it, although the forelegs are sometimes pictured as human. A Greek design from about 410 B.C. shows four centaurs pulling a chariot in what is apparently a comic performance, black-bearded heads above torsos that take the place of the heads of horses (Pickard-Cambridge [F], Fig. 77a,b,c). They have their hands behind their backs and appear to be captives of Herakles who drives the chariot. Perhaps in a performance each creature was played by two men, like the Balinese lion-*barong*, but the artist might only have "mythologized" single dancers. In art and mythology that preserves their history, it is apparent not only that the centaurs are representations of an alien people (Harrison [P], 384; Rose, 257), but of a shamanistic culture.

Centaurs are not known in Peloponesian art of the Mycenaean period (1580–1120 B.C.). They first appear, it seems, among the Babylonian Cassites and Hittites about 1350 B.C. (Baur, 2–3). The Hittite and Cassite centaurs often have small wings growing from their backs, a symbolism identifying them with the flight of the shaman's horse as trance vehicle. They have panther and leopard skins draped about them and use bows and arrows, indications that they are of a hunting people, perhaps alien in origin.

The centaur appears in Greek art itself early in the geometric period, possibly in the ninth century B.C., being figured in a style associated with the Hittites. These early vases show variations on a repeated stylized motif of a centaur with an upraised tree in his hand confronting a man armed with a double ax or a sword (Cook, II, 614–17). It is difficult to decide whether these designs represent a conflict between cultures or within a culture. Sometimes it seems as if the confrontation is amicably resolved and essentially symbolic, as in a design in which a centaur and a man both grasp a tree. What is certain, however, is that the tree the centaurs extend toward the men, or the tree they wield as a weapon, is their distinct "religion," the shamanistic world view itself, identified with the tree as vertical axis of the shaman's trance flight.

As the designs become more sophisticated, the tree theme remains; a centaur is shown about to uproot a tree or with a tree slung over his shoulder or wielding it as a weapon. Here, the centaurs are often shown battling among themselves. It is an image that derives, I believe, from the well-known practice of shamans fighting each other during, and by means of, their trances. The centaurs are also shown fighting naked men, the Lapiths or the followers of Herakles, on vases that picture the

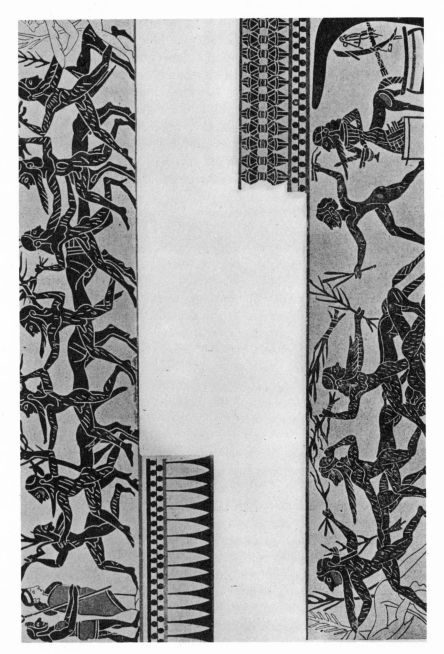

20. Centaurs being driven from Pholus' cave by Herakles, lower right.

myths of cultural contact and change.

In the course of the development of these designs, an interesting transformation in the conventions of style may be observed. The trees that are at first shown uprooted and whole often become huge branches, more realistic as weapons than entire trees, and then they frequently become replaced with vines used as weapons. The vines are drawn in the same way as those that wind sinuously in the background of other satyr and centaur designs, and they are precisely the conventionalized vines of Dionysus. We have noted that the vines of Dionysianism are representations of trance and hallucination. Their use by the centaurs as weapons is a natural extension of this image. Figuratively, the trance is shown to have been the weapon of the centaurs, just as it was literally the weapon of the shaman. Vase pictures associate the centaurs directly with the full range of Dionysian subjects. One centaur is pictured as having torn a fawn to pieces like a maenad or like Dionysus. Centaurs are often shown together with satyrs, and one vase shows both "hairy" and "smooth" centaurs, just as there were also these two types of satyrs.

Mythology tells us that the centaurs were a race of beings that was born of a delusion. Their etiology was traced from Ixion's attempt to possess Hera. Zeus replaced her with a cloud shaped in her likeness, with which Ixion copulated, and the cloud (Nephele) gave birth to the being, part horse, part man, from which the race of centaurs sprang (Cook, I, 198). The cloud was an illusion as hallucination, like the figure of Dionysus formed of the "ether that surrounds the world" shown to Hera to deceive her, or like the figure of "gleaming air" that appears to Pentheus, or like the figure behind Xanthos, and so on. Ixion's act was also like the delusionary copulations of the trance flight. The deception of Ixion was metaphysical—and sociological. The myths state that the shamanists (Ixion) had desired divinity, but had never reached it nor participated in it, and had experienced only illusion. They were rash to desire one of the Olympian pantheon.

In punishment for his presumption, Ixion was bound to a winged and flaming wheel and set to spin forever in the sky (or later, in the underworld); an image that reproduced in perpetuity the spinning dance of the shaman and the terrible price of insanity associated with his trances. It was the price paid for "reaching the sky." In one vase picture, Athena (the wisdom of rational thought) is shown bringing the wheel to which Ixion will be bound, while two other gods hold him. He was, in fact, bound there by the whole Olympian pantheon (Cook, I, 200).

Ixion's progeny, the centaurs, representing the shamanists, are shown in further conflict with the Olympians in myths that detail both their suppression and their influence.

Cheiron, the wisest of the centaurs and their leader, he who had taught the art of medicine to Asclepius, received from Herakles a wound that could not be healed. This was, perhaps, the psychic wound that already characterized shamanistic practice, and Cheiron gladly gave up his immortality to Prometheus, who would himself suffer, but in a new way, under the bonds of rationalism. Cheiron's wound was an accident; Herakles had aimed at one of the unruly centaurs, not at their wisdom. This seems to have been intended to indicate that the new gods and their world order had, in effect, superseded shamanism unintentionally, outmoded it; that it was, abstractly speaking, immortal; that it had, in part, contributed to the culture; but that it could not, and should not, sustain itself at the price of the psychic suffering it was paying for its practices. Herakles, opponent of the shamanistic centaurs, had long since disposed of the serpents of trance flight, having strangled a pair of them while still in his cradle.

The licentiousness of the centaurs was a necessary postulation of didacticism. The battles with the centaurs were caused by their interruption of two weddings, that of Herakles and that of the Lapith god, Kaineus. In both cases the bride, whom the centaurs tried to abduct, was named Hippodameia, "female tamer of horses." She represented the ethos of the society that would tame *these* horses, the horses of the trance. Kaineus seems to have been a deified leader in Thessaly, and was clearly a shaman—or shamaness. He had been a woman, was raped by Poseidon, chose to be transformed into a man and then worshiped only his spear, which he set up in the ground like the vertical axis. Also descended from Ixion, Kaineus was invulnerable to weapons, but the centaurs won the battle against the Lapiths and hammered him into the earth with the shamanistic fir tree.

The characteristic of drunkenness attributed to the centaurs and to the satyrs derived from a specific didactic symbolism. Wine was represented as the cause of the battle between Herakles and the centaurs at Pholus's cave. Pholus refused to break the seal on an ancient amphora of wine just so that his guest, Herakles, might be served, saying that the wine was the common property of all the centaurs. Herakles insisted, observing that Zeus had wanted it saved for this particular occasion, and when the wine was poured its aroma immediately attracted all the other centaurs, who stormed the cave in a fury.

It is apparent that the wine symbolizes the ancient religion, the shamanistic wisdom and world view, that the centaurs wanted to keep for themselves. The battle occurs when Herakles, the representative of the Olympian world view, gets it opened to him. We know that wine as intoxication was a symbol of the ecstatic Dionysianism of which the centaurs were ancient creatures. The centaurs fought to save their religious experience, not their wine, but popular mythologizers attributed drunkenness to them on this account. In a similar manner, Silenus was made drunk on wine to learn the secrets of his ancient wisdom, probably a reference to its ecstatic nature. He was the eponym of the silens, a type of trance horse shown as aged, and the leader of the satyrs in the satyr plays, in which he then came to be represented as drunken.

The rapes and abductions attributed to satyrs and centaurs by myth were therefore didactic metaphor, representations of the forced seductions of a particular world view seen from the perspective of a specific attitude toward it. The drunkenness of their world view was clearly a disparagement of trance, based on wine as a symbol of religious experience, as was the licentiousness of the satyrs, and their unruly nature derived from the internecine warfare of the shamans pictured as centaurs battling among themselves.

The satyrs and centaurs represented the archaic, shamanistic level of Dionysianism. The attitude toward them expressed in their mythology was not actually overly biased. It was, in a sense, an accurate history. But it had an inherent aspect of humor, even of ridicule. Thus, in the process of time, the satyrs became mythologized by parody. When they came to be performers in satyr plays, it was natural that they should turn this same satire and parody back upon the Olympian pantheon in general and upon its particular emissary, Herakles, the antagonist of the horse-man in the mythology that had, in effect, slandered them. The myths of Herakles, subordinator of the primitive, already contained humor, and he was also frequently parodied by Dorian farce. This type of blasphemous metaphysical farce is maintained by socioreligious sanction and represents an archetypal level in the development of comedy. The satyrs became "trapped" in this mode, as it were.

Satire and parody were not the only weapons in society's reformation of archaic Dionysianism. The battle between Apollonian and Dionysian was symbolized as a war of musical modes. Conclusions were presented didactically and unambiguously. Athena had given up the double flute of her ancient origins on becoming the image of rational thought, but it was picked up by the satyr, Marsyas, who continued to play this Dionysian instrument, much to her displeasure. Marsyas was then defeated by Apollo in a famous contest of musical modes. As a consequence, he was flayed alive, and his skin was hung on a pine tree, the world-tree of his shamanistic origins. The goat-satyr Pan was also defeated by Apollo in a similar musical contest.

One of the major myths in the revision of Dionysianism was that concerning Orpheus and his dismemberment by the maenads. Significantly enough, the Orphic movement originated around 600 B.C., contemporaneous with Arion's reform of the dithyrambic trance dance. The Orphics worshiped Dionysus, and Orpheus was said to have been a follower or priest of Dionysus (Guthrie, 82). But the musical instrument he played so well was the lyre of Apollo, not the pipes and cymbals of Dionysianism. Orphism sought to mediate the polarity between the Dionysian and the Apollonian.

The descent of Orpheus to the underworld to bring back his wife, Eurydice, has been observed to derive from a shamanistic pattern (Eliade, 392). That is, it relates to the trance marriage in another world to a spirit wife. The Orphic variation of this pattern as an apparently purposeful negation of it is interesting. Eurydice dies from stepping on a snake, again the snake of trance flight. Orpheus fails to bring her back; he cannot keep his spirit wife. He seems, therefore, to have founded the institution of homosexuality (Rose, 255). The sex change of the shaman clearly provided a precedent.

Orpheus, it was said, went to Thrace for the purpose of suppressing sacrificial murder there. As noted, Thrace was an area of shamanistic influence upon Dionysianism. The sacrificial murder Orpheus intended to suppress was undoubtedly the dismemberment and boiling associated with shamanic initiation. But this representative of Dionysus met an analogous, and distinctly incongruous, fate; he was hacked to pieces by the maenads, who were also followers of Dionysus. This was unlike the fate of Pentheus, as Guthrie observed, since the women used various weapons, thus making "it clear that he is not taking the part of a victim in a Bacchic orgy" (Guthrie, 49). The murder of Orpheus by the maenads, relating indirectly to dismemberment of Zagreus-Dionysus by the Titans, seems to have been an intentional symbolism in a conscious, conceptual revision of Dionysianism.

Orpheus, in fact, seems to have been torn apart only so that his severed head might continue to sing and prophesy. What it sang was the music of Apollo, "music regulated and chaste," as Plutarch called it, composed of rational, mathematical harmonies. It was the music of the mode of the mind—even of the head severed from its body—not music of the mode of the body, of the god born from the thigh of Zeus, nor of "the dithyrambic strains laden with emotion." The myth of Orpheus presents him as a martyr to the Dionysian mode, and it opposes to Bacchic violence a style personified by a figure with a "calm and civilized air" who was "always on the side of civilization and the arts of peace" (Guthrie, 42, 40). The rending or *sparagmos* of Orpheus was purely a didactic invention.

It is ironic, in this regard, to note that by 425 B.C. the satyrs singing in contests of dithyrambs at the Panathenea were accompanying themselves on the lyre, the instrument of Apollo and Orpheus (Pickard-Cambridge, Ia).

Chapter VI

EUROPE: MUMMERS' PLAY AND FOLK THEATER

A particular type of folk play, known as the mummers' play, is found in European cultures as divergent as those of England, Spain, Germany, Greece, and Russia, and seems to be the survival of some type of ritual or enactment characteristic of the aboriginal culture. Interpretation of the mummers' play has been the particular purview of vegetation-cycle theorists. The typical definition states that it is "a survival of the primitive Ritual Pattern, combining the twin elements of (a) the Combat of the Seasons and (b) the Death-and-Resurrection of the god of fertility" (Gaster, 64). Mummers' plays were supposed to have represented the agon that found a place in both comedy and tragedy, according to the theories of Cornford and Murray. We are told that these plays "are all seasonal," and such things as "certainly one of the themes of this combat is the ritual imitation of the death of the sun in winter and its rebirth in spring" (Brody, 3, 53). There is, in fact, no evidence either in the form of the plays or in their times of appearance that indicate that they are or were seasonal. The same play can be performed at any time during the year. Chambers would seem to have known this when he held that the mummers' plays were "originally seasonal" but that they "have been curiously dislocated in the process of adaptation to superimposed calendars" (Chambers [F], 221). I have written on this subject elsewhere, analyzing the statistics of appearance, and there is nothing in them that cannot be accounted for by the nature of the superimposed calendars (Kirby).

The mummers' play begins with a space being cleared in the midst of an audience so that a naive introduction may be given by one of the performers, a "presenter." Two characters then brag in turn about their exploits and they stage a mock combat in which one of them is killed or wounded. These characters are frequently called St. George (or King George) and the Turkish Knight, or they might be Bold Bonaparte and Captain Slasher. The list of names designating the combatants is extensive (Tiddy, 11), and it is apparent that the identities are topical and variable, mutable rather than definitive. From them it would be difficult to postulate credibly the identities of the "original" combatants. There is no apparent basis for discriminating between victor and vanquished; the number of plays in which the "hero" is slain or wounded is equivalent to the number of those in which the antagonist is slain or wounded (Tiddy, 12). Sometimes the vanquished is named for a national hero and the victor is a foreigner. What becomes apparent is that the symbolic identity of the person slain or wounded is secondary to the basic function of the combat; to supply someone on whom the doctor can practice his miraculous cure. For invariably, a doctor then enters, brags about his travels and his abilities at healing and proceeds to cure or bring to life again the wounded or slain man. Often the combat and the curing are then repeated again or several times more. When this is concluded, various minor characters enter, and each has a brief speech indicating who he is. The performance ends with a collection of money from the audience and with a song.

The cure, not the combat, is the basic element in the performance. It has been apparent that the doctor in the mummers' plays "is the medicine man of primitive races" (Tiddy, 76). In specific cases the play shows evidence of derivation from the cure as practiced by the shaman. We have noted that the latter was achieved with the extraction from the patient of some object representing the "pain." In the mummers' play this cure is often retained in the form of a comic anomaly. In a performance from Austria and in several from the British Isles, when a combatant is killed or wounded in the sword fight he is cured by having a tooth drawn, and an elk's or horse's or donkey's tooth is exhibited to the spectators. More commonly, a simple comic device that might possibly have derived from this is employed; a large bolus, a pill that could not possibly be swallowed, is exhibited to the spectators as the means of cure, just as the shaman had triumphantly exhibited the pain he had extracted. In at least one version, the patient is cured by being blown up with air through a tube, a circumstance that seems to derive from a

shamanic practice of sometimes extracting a pain by suction through a
tube.

An old tooth was one of the objects that might be exhibited as the
pain by the Sema Naga shaman of India (Charles, 106). In a similar
manner, in the Snowshill mummers' play the Doctor draws the tooth of
a slain man and exhibits a horse's tooth he has hidden in his hand, to
the exclamation of "Look, look ladies and gentlemen; more like a
horse's, elephant's or camel's tooth than a Christian's!" This would
seem to have been suggested by the common practice by the shaman of
hiding in his own mouth the object he pretended to extract from the
patient. The extraction of a tooth in the mummers' play would be the
nearest civilized equivalent to extracting a pain from the patient, as well
as being a parody of this practice.

It is possible, of course, that these are analogies and not direct deriv-
ations. However, it is clear that the concept of the pain as materializa-
tion of the disease has led elsewhere to transformation of the curing
seance into performance in which such magical objects are directly
related to magical "deaths" and revivals. In the Kwakiutl winter ceremonies, a performer "kills" himself and others with a wormlike object
representing the disease, and he and the others are then "resurrected"
(Boas [S], 485). The medicine rite of the Winnebago, Pawnee, and
many other tribes, is characterized by shooting magic shells into others
and by swallowing them in order to effect a series of miraculous deaths
and resurrections (Radin [R]). In a masquerade of the Ogoni of
Nigeria, a mask called Doctor brags about his medicines, but they kill
the patient who must then be restored to life (G. Jones, 192). The
bragging of the doctor is also characteristic of the mummers' plays.

The speeches of the Doctor in the mummers' play deal with two
themes: his travels and his abilities at curing. These themes were based
upon, and derive from, the travels of the shamans' soul during trance
which he elaborated in his songs and narratives. The bragging of the
Doctor is equivalent to that of the shaman, a characteristic which, when
not explicit (as it most often was), was implicit in his essentially fantastic narratives of his journeys during trance. The Doctor often brags
of medical knowledge gained through "going abroad" to study, again
indicating a superficial adaptation of the form to civilization. In the
mummers' plays we find echoes and evidence of reference to the shaman's trance journeys and of the fantastic and garbled manner of his
speaking. In some versions the Doctor has traveled to Cockaigne, clearly
a realm of the imaginary, or he may have gained his ability in a voyage

to the bottom of the sea, equivalent with the shaman's initiatory descent to his spirit ancestors. In the Pace-Eggers Play, for example, the Doctor has traveled:

> From Timbuctoo to the Atlantic Ocean, Ninety degrees below the bottom where I saw Houses built of rounds of beef, slated with pancakes; roasted pigs running up and down the streets with knives and forks sticking in their teeth, crying "Here's a living! Who'll die?"   (E. Wilson, 40)

Another play seems to provide a mocking reference to shamanic ascent and initiatory dismemberment.

> *Lady*: How came you to be a Doctor?
> *Doctor*: By my travels.
> *Lady*: Where have *you* travelled?
> *Doctor*: Up hill where *you* couldn't get.
> *Lady*: How did *you* get there?
> *Doctor*: Cut my hands and feet off, threw them up and went up after them.
>
> (*Journal of the English Folk Dance and Song Society*, 5 [December 1974], 87)

The Doctor has gained his particular knowledge in strange ways. The form of expression seems to be that of a basic mocking or parodic intent obliquely referencing the shamanic experience.

> *The Old Witch says*
> Where have you learnt your skill, Docter?
> *The Docter*
> I have traveled for it.
> *The Old Witch says*
> Where have you traveled?
> *The Docter says*
> I have traveled from my Old Grandmother's Fireside, to her Bread and Cheese Cupboard Door, And there had many a rare piece of Bread and Cheese.   (Chambers [F], 95–6)

More usually, the Doctor's travels are wider in scope, such as "From France, from Spain, from Rome I come./ I've travelled all parts of

Christendom," which is typical. In a similar manner, the shaman's trance travels extended to "other" worlds, but also covered "wide geographical areas—real, known regions" (Lommel, 69). The Doctor associates himself with the place of performance. Having gained valuable knowledge on his travels, he has returned in the nick of time, as it were.

> In comes I, Doctor Hero. I was borned at home: I have travelled many parts of the country and am well known at home.
>
> (Tiddy, 162)

As did the shaman, the Doctor brags about miraculous cures, such as that of the dog that he brings back to life after finding it on his way (his way "back") to the play.

> I went on a little bit further: I came to two little whipper snappers thrashing canary seeds: one gave a hard cut, the tother gen a driving cut, cut a sid through a wall nine foot wide kelled a little jed dog tother side. I went of the morroe about nine days after, picks up this little jied dog, romes my arm down his throat, turned him inside outards, sent him down Buckle Street barking ninety miles long and I followed after him.   (Tiddy, 168)

In a similar manner, the shaman's style of expression was often unintelligible and was sometimes thought of as a secret language. But these parallels are at a considerable remove from their source and retain only in general terms the context of the miraculous, of shamanism.

A more direct way of ascertaining the shamanistic origins of the mummers' play is by a consideration of the hobbyhorse that appears in it and in many other related performances such as the sword dances and Morris dances. The hobbyhorse, by clear association, gives us indication of the antiquity of the mummers' play in historical times and the extent of the basic phenomenon throughout Europe. Saint Augustine spoke out against the mummings, the "*sordissiman turpitudinem de hinnicula vel cervula*," in A.D. 395, as did Bishop Caesarius of Arles about A.D. 506. The Council of Auxerre, 573–603, decreed: "It is not allowed . . . to perform with a cervulus, a hobby-horse or to observe the giving of presents to demons." Again, about A.D. 750, Priminius decreed, "Do not process with Hobby-horses or calves on the Kalends." All of these proscriptions were apparently to little avail (Alford [D],

24, [S], 240). By 1200 the Church was resorting to tales such as that reported by a Dominican of a Mediterranean village regarding a boy disguised as a hobbyhorse who persisted in calling for "the usual play" until a fire sprang out of the ground and burned him up on the spot (Alford [D], 24).

The Padstow Horse, a unique feature of an ancient mumming from the north coast of Cornwall, is formed of a black sheath of tarred cloth that descends to the ground as a skirt from a hoop of this material, about five feet in diameter, at the player's shoulders. Rising above the center of the hoop is a black mask of a human face, while from the front of the hoop protrudes a small, grotesque carved head of a horse with a movable jaw. The unity or identification of horse and man are clearly shown. It would appear to be a relic of trance dancing which illustrates the merger of the trancer with a possessing consciousness that dominates and "rides" him. The spinning dance of the Padstow Horse would be a survival of spinning or circular dances used to induce trance in performances such as those of the Buryat shaman.

The Calusari ("little horses") of Rumania are (or were) ecstatic dancers who dance continuously from morning to dark for weeks at a time for the purpose of curing and exorcism. Toward the end of the nineteenth century, the first dancer carried a carved horse's head on a pole, an image like that associated with the dance in Cheshire, England. In the eighteenth century the first dancer wore a stork's-head mask, the beak of which could be moved with a string (Vuia, 97–98). As noted, both horse and bird are vehicles of the shaman's trance flight. The hobbyhorse in the Bakovian dances related to those of the Calusari is an interesting representation. It has around its head a paper hoop with pictures of the sun, moon, and stars on it (Vuia, 105). The shaman's drum also often has just such pictures (Czaplica, 220). The attachment to the horse is logical. The shaman "traveled" by means of his drum and it was thought of as his "horse." (Eliade, 171). The hoop on the Bakovian horse showed the trance realm toward which it was flying. Apparently for the same reason, the hobbyhorse dancers of Mallorca wear eagle feathers (Sachs, 134), and the ancient mummers' hobbyhorse of Wales, made from a horse skull raised on a pole, is not called a horse, but rather *Aderyn Pig Lwyd*, "Bird with the Grey Beak" (Alford [S], 223). In the same way, bird and shaman have merged in the person of the "beaked Fool," the translation of the Cantabrian *Zorromoco* and the Basque *Katximorro*, and beaked disguises characterize the followers of Berta who run in the *Schnabelperchten* (Alford [S], 223).

In the mummers' plays the shaman's trance horse may be represented simply by the horse that the Doctor is said to have ridden and that he appears to leave outside when he enters. But it is indicated in more explicit ways as well. The hobbyhorse and the Doctor have been identified as originally one character, on the basis of the resemblance of the horse's travels with those of the Doctor (Chambers [F], 30). In the Ormskirk play it is said of the hobbyhorse that: "He's travelled through Ireland, France, and Spain, / And now he's back in Old England again" (Chambers [F], 30). This is also a typical phrasing used to describe the travels of the Doctor.

Other characters are used in the mummers' plays to represent the Doctor's horse, and often he is carried in on the back of one of them. In Greece the Doctor will not come in without a "horse," and an Old Woman then carries him in (Chambers [F], 30). In the Longborough play, Beelzebub is known as the "old woman" but also called "the doctor's horse," and the Doctor rides in on his back. Beelzebub and the Old Woman appear to be duplications of the Doctor in terms of the trance-horse schema and also as variations on the shamanic identity. In the Longborough play the Doctor mounts his horse again before performing the cure. There is, in short, always much byplay concerned with the Doctor's horse, even when a hobbyhorse does not appear.

The combat in the Revesby play is between the fool and the hobbyhorse, with the latter being killed (Chambers [M], 208). A hobbyhorse is killed in the Basque masquerade, and, at Goathland in Yorkshire, the necessary death is produced when a rider falls from the back of a hobbyhorse (Chambers [F], 213). In Central Asia, the ecstatic Pamir dancers tie the typical horse-headed stick in front of their bodies "and, after much whipping, 'die' " (Sachs, 338). These "deaths" show that the central image of the mummers' play, a "death and resurrection," derives from the temporary "deaths" of the trance state.

> . . . it is clear that it is *the shaman himself who becomes the dead man* (or the animal spirit, or the god, etc.), in order to demonstrate his real ability to ascend to the sky or descend to the underworld. In this light, a common explanation for all these groups of facts seems possible; in a sense, they represent the periodical repetition (that is, begun over again at each new séance) of the shaman's death and resurrection.   (Eliade, 35)

Examples of this death and resurrection having become a performance in primitive cultures are cited above in regard to throwing a magic object related to the "pain." In the mummers' play it is often said that the victim in the combat is not dead after all, but only "in a trance." In these instances the experience of the patient duplicates that of the trance Doctor, rather than the converse. With such duplication it becomes apparent why it makes little difference whether the protagonist or the antagonist is killed or wounded in the mummers' play.

The parallel of symbolic identity between the Doctor-shaman and the patient, as well as the doubling, the identification, of the Doctor-shaman and his horse, has led in the mummers' plays to a form in which other basic characters, such as the Fool, the Man-Woman, and Beelzebub may be seen as further doubling of the identity of the shaman.

In the Revesby play, which is combined with a Morris dance, it is the Fool that is killed. He kneels and the dancers form a "lock" about his neck (or over his head) with their swords. The Fool looks at the "lock" through his spectacles, and it is here known as a "glass," that is, a mirror. In it the Fool sees his own face and understands that he is to be killed. He draws up his will, is killed by the dancers, and is then brought to life again. This is repeated several times, with variations (Chambers [M], 208).

The "lock" of swords which is also a "mirror" is, it appears to me, a symbolization of gripping or seizure in trance possession and also of the actual mirror that often plays a part in inducing shamanic trance, as we have noted. The Fool in the Revesby play is then the Doctor-shaman, and his "death" the trance. The leader of the Calusari ("little horses") also derives from this source. A comic figure, masked and humorously dressed, he nevertheless is supposed to have magic powers over the other Calusari, and carries a sword and a whip, hitting out around the dancers to drive away evil spirits (Vuia, 97). Essentially, this would not have varied much from the shamanic function of "proctoring" trance dancers. Here, too, we find the enactments of death and revival derived from the shamanistic seance pattern. The Fool of the Calusari of Muscel is killed and then brought to life again, and in the similar Rumanian *boricza* two dumb men or fools fight, with one being killed and then brought back to life (Vuia, 98, 101).

The Fool in the Bassingham play brags that, "I slew Ten men with a Seed of Mustard, / Ten thousand with an old Crush'd Toad." This use of parodied medicines (medicines of witchcraft) in a boast further links the Fool with the Doctor as a parody of the shaman. The Fool in this play is killed in the combat, and one might well assume that this form of boasting and this form of combat, with the shaman-Doctor as a participant, preceded the boasting and combat of the armed knights.

Most of the other characters in the mummers' play can also be derived from parodies of the shaman. In several plays Beelzebub has also gone on journeys, just as the Doctor has, and he appears as the Doctor's horse. In a similar manner, the Man-Woman is significant as a representation-as-parody of the shamanic sex change. The Calusari wear female costume, wreathe their heads with flowers, cover their faces with white veils, and speak with women's voices (when they speak at all), a convention which is something more than parody.

The shaman's assistant appears in the mummers' plays as the character most often called Jack Finney. The function of this assistant, the shaman's "talker," would be that of the presenter in the mummers' plays. Indeed, among the names by which this presenter has been known is that of "talking man" (Chambers [F], 94). The shaman's "talker" often received half of his fee, a fact that may be considered in relation to the collection as a feature of the mummers' plays.

The primary factor in the transition from shamanistic ritual to entertainment was the contact with an alien culture that caused the aboriginal beliefs and practices to lose their credibility. In reconstructing the process of development, it would appear that at first the disbelieved "empty form" was continued intact, but was thought of as a parody so as to protect the associated beliefs and practices. Later, this aspect of parody was emphasized further, elaborated in the characters duplicating the shaman and in the farcical treatment of the curing. Entertainment, which had always been an element in the seance, became its primary function in these performances. Evidence of this development may be observed even today.

When Siberian shamans perform an exhibition at the request of the Russians, they remove their caps so that the performance no longer contains the power, the efficacy, that is thought to be hidden in the caps. Donner reports: "When I questioned them about this, they told me that, shamanizing without a cap, they were deprived of all real power and hence the whole ceremony was only a parody principally intended to amuse the audience" (Eliade, 154). The protective aspect of this "parody" should be noted, the removal of the beliefs from criticism by skeptics, and also the financial motives involved in performing in this way. Two reasons, the economic and the social, must be considered basic in the perpetuation of the shamanistic seance as performance when it was confronted with disbelief. The shaman and his associates endeavored not to lose their means of support when their actual services became discredited, and the people hesitated to give up their basic form of entertainment.

Many of the folk customs that are related to the mummers' play involve a *quête*, a procession that begs for gifts, and in them we may study various representations of society's attitude toward the shaman as seen from the point of view of the "new culture" that replaced the shamanistic. At their simplest level these folk customs present the shaman as a beggar and a butt, a means of collecting gifts. Observances in Bavaria preserve the spinning dance of the shaman, but the psychopomp has become a quack.

> . . . a boy or lad is swathed in the yellow blossom of the broom, the dark green twigs of the firs, and other foliage. Thus attired he is known as the Quack and goes from door to door, whirling about in the dance, while an appropriate song is chanted and his companions levy contributions   (Frazer, 121)

In the Northern Highlands of the British Isles, the Shetlands and Orkneys, the shaman, as a combination of horse and clown, became a man wrapped in cow's hide and pummeled as the basis of a *quête*.

> [He] was beaten with resounding blows. They all ran three times round the house, and sang improvised verses at the door. This cow's hide may well have been intended for a horse's hide, for in the Shetlands that is what it was called. The beaten man here was "a carrying horse." He fulfilled the double role of Horse and Clown.
> (Alford [S], 229)

The horse as prophet, a shamanic function, is found in the Isle of Man Laare Van ritual (Brody, 64).

The multiplication of the shaman's identity undoubtedly began in protective parody, a knowingness on the part of those who knew, as it were, even though the personifications represented him as foolish, evil or insane, as the Fool, the Devil, or the Wild Man. This in turn provided the basis for rejective parody, a caricature of both the "old way" and the "new culture," and for the fundamental anarchic spirit of the mummings known throughout Europe.

In the performance at Combe Martin in North Devon, for example, a grotesquely masked Earl of Rone, padded with straw and wearing a string of biscuits around his neck, was attended by a squad of equally grotesque "grenadiers." The Earl hid, and the grenadiers searched for him. There then followed an interesting variation of the deaths and resurrections that the mummers' play had derived from the shamans' trance.

> [The grenadiers] fired a volley, caught [the Earl] and setting him on a donkey, face to the tail, took him back to the village. Here the Hobby and the Fool met him. Now and again the grenadiers fired volleys, when the Earl would fall off his steed and lie wounded on the ground. The soldiers exulted: the Hobby and the Fool lamented. The latter then replaced the Earl on donkey-back and the procession proceeded. This . . . scene was repeated again and again for hours.   (Alford [S], 236)

The old and the new cultures are both parodied in terms of the seance pattern, but even the Earl, like the hobbyhorse and the Fool, derived from the shaman. Alford notes that the hiding, search, and discovery of the Earl "is an exact analogy with the hiding, capture and death of the Candlemas Bear at Arles" (Alford [S], 237). Thus another identity can be added to those based on the shaman. It is a logical one, since the shaman in the seance often appeared to transform himself into a bear and other animals. But the pattern of hiding, capture, and death relates these to other performances throughout Europe.

Frazer describes a folk enactment from Saxony and Thüringen called "chasing the Wild Man out of the bush" or "fetching the Wild Man out of the Wood," as follows:

> A young fellow is enveloped in leaves or moss and called the Wild Man. He hides in the wood and the other lads of the village go out to seek him. They find him, lead him captive out of the wood, and fire at him with blank muskets. He falls like dead to the ground, but a lad dressed as a doctor bleeds him, and he comes to life again. At this they rejoice, and, binding him fast on a waggon, take him to the village, where they tell all the people how they caught the Wild Man. At every house they receive a gift.   (Frazer, 304)

This figure was not a "spirit of vegetation," as Frazer believed. The shaman had become a Wild Man, driven away from civilization, and a "new doctor" was there to bleed him and effect the shamanic "re-surrection" when he was captured.

These examples could be multiplied almost indefinitely. We have a fairly clear indication that a shamanistic substratum informed and produced not only the mummers' plays and mummings but much of the whole spectrum of folk customs and festival observances that characterized the survival of the primitive throughout Europe. It is apparent in regard to the mummers' plays that one is not "justified in classing them as forms of a folk drama in which the resurrection of the year is symbolized" (Chambers [M], I, 202). Nor do they "seem to find their natural explanation in the facts of agricultural worship" (Chambers [F], 207).

The effect upon the development of drama in medieval Europe exercised by folk performances should not be underestimated. Mummings and related dances contributed much to the interludes which evolved into full dramatic forms. The whole spectrum of folk performance existed from earliest times, presenting at least a rudimentary form of dramatic enactment. From this, or from professional actors influenced by it, there developed a secular drama of stereotypical comic scenes which came to form a part of the medieval religious drama. The evolution of the religious drama from an origin in the antiphonal choirs of the *quem quaeritis* trope is well known, but the role of secular dramatic activity in this development is a subject of controversy. Some would understand that the latin choral responses with minimal dramatic activity staged within the church eventually led directly to the vast, outdoor, vernacular cycles encompassing the history of mankind, with the former structuring the latter, in an essentially hermetic process of development. Others would question this view.

Among the stereotypical scenes which gave form to the developing religious drama is one that involved a doctor, and "it is certainly most interesting that the speech he yells out in some of the folk plays is nearly identical with the speech of the Mercator in a twelfth-century Easter Play from Tours, in a thirteenth-century play called *Les trois Maries*, in the Alsfelder Passion Play from twelfth-century Germany, and other scenes of the unguent merchant" (Hunningher, 102).

Robert Stumpfl's *Kultspiele des Germanen als Ursprung des mittel-alterlichen Dramas* (1936) used the quack doctor as a survival of the witch doctor in a theory which postulated primitive antecedents in Germanic initiation ritual which had prefigured and suggested enactment of the *quem quaeritis* trope. The theory itself seems to be incorrect; however, it "has the merit of having thrown into sharp relief a defect in earlier literary historians, namely, their neglect of the indigenous religious forms and beliefs prevalent among the Germanic peoples at the time of and after their conversions" (Pascal, 373). The point is that folk dramas were there at the origins of drama and the secular performances seem to have been instrumental in the creation of drama. It is quite certain that it is in those areas from which we have most evidence of secular dramatic activity that most of the [religious] manuscripts come.

It is very doubtful whether the Easter tropes, and their counterparts at Christmas, could ever have led to the development of drama in any real sense of the term. The severe restrictions on the characters and their actions prevented any real expansion beyond a few tricks of staging and verbal variation.   (Jackson, 283)

It is impossible not to connect the growth of pagan and secular, humorous and realistic elements in the religious drama with the removal of the representations to church door or market-place, the increasing participation of lay actors, the use of the vernacular: in general, with the development of the towns.   (Pascal, 383)

Again, however diffused its influence might have been, a shamanism absorbed into folk culture lay at the origins of theatre.

LIST OF WORKS CITED

Adedeji, J. A. "The Origin of the Yoruba Masque Theatre: The Use of Ifa Divination Corpus as Historical Evidence," *African Notes* (Ibadan), 6:1 (1970).

Alagoa, E. J. "Delta Masquerades," *Nigeria Magazine*, 93 (1967).

Alford, Violet. (S) "Some Hobby Horses of Great Britain," *Journal of the English Folk Dance and Song Society*, 3 (December 1939).

——. (D) *Sword Dance and Drama*. Philadelphia, 1965.

Anisimov, A. F. (C) "Cosmological Concepts of the Peoples of the North," *Studies in Siberian Shamanism*. Ed. Henry N. Michael. Toronto, 1963.

——. (S) "The Shaman's Tent of the Evenks and the Origin of the Shamanistic Rite," *Studies in Siberian Shamanism*. Ed. Henry N. Michael. Toronto, 1963.

Araki, James T. *The Ballad-Drama of Medieval Japan*. Berkeley, 1964.

Arasaratnam, S. *Indian Festivals in Malaya*. Kuala Lumpur, 1966.

Arieti, Silvano, ed. *American Handbook of Psychiatry*. New York, 1959–1966. 3 vols.

Arlington, L. C. *The Chinese Drama: From the Earliest Times until Today*. New York, 1966. (1930).

Arnott, Peter. *The Theatres of Japan*. London, 1969.

Asaji, Nabori. *A Philosophy of the Japanese Noh Drama: An Excerpt from my Book of Noh*. Tokushima, 1964.

Aston, W. G., trans. *Nihongi*. (Introduction.) c. 1896; rpt. London, 1956.

Bancroft, Hubert Howe. *The Native Races*, vol. 1 of *The Works of Hubert Howe Bancroft*. San Francisco, 1886. 5 vols.

Bandelier, Adolf F. *The Delight Makers*. New York, 1954.

Bather, A. G. "The Problem of the Bacchae," *Journal of Hellenistic Studies*, 14 (1894).

Baur, Paul V. C. *Centaurs in Ancient Art: The Archaic Period*. Berlin, 1912.

Beattie, John, and John Middleton, eds. *Spirit Mediumship and Society in Africa*. New York, 1969.

Belo, Jane. (B) *Traditional Balinese Culture*. New York, 1970.

———. (T) *Trance in Bali*. New York, 1960.

Bhat, G. K. The *Vidūsaka*. Ahmedabad, 1959.

Blackmun, Barbara, and Matthew Schoffeleers. "Masks of Malawi," *African Arts*, 5:4 (Summer 1972).

Blau, Harold. "Function and False Faces," *Journal of American Folklore*, 79 (October–December 1966).

Boas, Franz. (E) "The Eskimo of Baffin Land and Hudson Bay," *Bulletin of the American Museum of Natural History*, 15 (1901).

———. (K) *Kwakiutl Ethnography*. Chicago, 1966.

———. (S) "The Social Organization and the Secret Societies of the Kwakiutl Indians," *Report of the United States National Museum for 1895*.

Brandon, James R. *On Thrones of Gold, Three Javanese Shadow Plays*. Cambridge, Massachusetts, 1970.

Brody, Alan. *The English Mummers and their Plays: Traces of Ancient Mystery*. Philadelphia, 1969.

Brown, Ivor. *First Player: The Origin of Drama*. New York, 1928.

Brown, John P. *The Darvishes, or Oriental Spiritualism*. Ed. H. R. Rose. 1968. (1868).

Brown, Norman O. *Hermes the Thief: The Evolution of a Myth*. New York, 1947.

Butterworth, E. A. S. *Some Traces of the Pre-Olympian World in Greek Literature and Myth*. Berlin, 1966.

Chamberlain, Basil Hall, trans. *Ko-ji-ki*. c. 1882; rpt. Kobe, 1932.

Chambers, E. K. (F) *The English Folk-Play*. Oxford, 1933.

———. (M) *The Medieval Stage*. 2 vols. Oxford, 1903.

Charles, Lucille Hoerr. "Drama in Shaman Exorcism," *Journal of American Folklore*, 66 (1953).

——. (R) "Regeneration through Drama at Death," *Journal of American Folklore*, 59 (1946).

Chittenden, Jacqueline. "The Master of Animals," *Hesperia,* 16:2 (1947).

Chiu-yao, Huang. "Appendix: A Brief Consideration of the Outstanding Characteristics of the Chinese Drama," George Kin Leung, ed. *Mei-Lan-Fang: Foremost Actor of China*. Shanghai, 1929.

Chu, C. T. "An Anatomy of Yuan Drama," *Chinese Culture*, 11:2 (1970).

Clark, J. P. "Aspects of Nigerian Drama," *Nigerian Magazine*, 89 (June 1966).

Classical and Folk Dances of India. Bombay, 1963. Pagination not continuous.

Colson, Elizabeth. "Spirit Possession among the Tonga of Zambia," John Beattie and John Middleton, eds. *Spirit Mediumship and Society in Africa*. New York, 1970.

Cook, Arthur Bernard. *Zeus: A Study in Ancient Religion*. 3 vols. Cambridge, England, 1914–1940.

Cornford, Francis Macdonald. *The Origin of Attic Comedy*. Garden City, 1914.

Crump, James I. "The Elements of Yüan Opera," *Journal of Asian Studies*, 17 (1958).

——. (Y) "Yüan-Pen, Yüan Drama's Rowdy Ancestor," *Literature East and West*, 14:4 (1970).

Curtis, Edward S. *The North American Indian*. 20 vols. New York, 1915.

Czaplicka, M. A. *Aboriginal Siberia: A Study in Social Anthropology*. Oxford, 1914.

Daniélou, Alain. *Hindu Polytheism*. New York, 1964.

de Groot, J. J. M. *The Religious System of China*. Taipei, 1964. 6 vols. Reference to Vol. 6.

de Kleen, Tyra. *Mudrās: The Ritual Hand-Poses of the Buddha Priests and the Shiva Priests of Bali*. New Hyde Park, New York, 1970.

Devi, Ragini. *Dance Dialects of India*. Delhi and London, 1972.

Dikshitar, V. R. Ramachandra, trans. and ed. *The Silappadikāram*. London, 1939.

Diószegi, Vilmos. *Tracing Shamans in Siberia: The Story of an Ethnographical Research Expedition*. Trans. Anita Rajkay Babó. New York, 1968.

Dodds, E.R. ed. (B) *Euripides Bacchae*. 2d ed. Oxford, 1960.

————. *The Greeks and the Irrational*. Boston, 1957.

D. W. M. "Oshogbo Celebrates Festival of Shango," *Nigeria Magazine* (Lagos), 40 (1953).

Eliade, Mircea. *Shamanism: Archaic Techniques of Ecstasy*. New York, 1964.

Elliot, Alan J. A. *Chinese Spirit-Medium Cults in Singapore*. New York, 1955.

Else, Gerald F. *The Origin and Early Form of Greek Tragedy*. Cambridge, Massachusetts, 1965.

Elwin, Verrier. *The Muria and their Ghotul*. Oxford, 1947.

Epton, Nina. "The Quivering Wand," Stewart Wavell, Audrey Butt, Nina Epton, *Trances*. London 1966.

————. (T) "Trance in the Shadows," Stewart Wavell, Audrey Butt, Nina Epton, *Trances*. London, 1966.

Fairchild, William P. "Shamanism in Japan," *Folklore Studies*, 21 (1962).

Farnell, Lewis Richard. *The Cults of the Greek States*. 5 vols. Oxford, 1909.

Fergusson, Erna. "Laughing Priests," *Theatre Arts Monthly*, 17:8 (August 1933).

Firth, Raymond. "Ritual and Drama in Malay Spirit Mediumship," *Comparative Studies in Society and History*, 9 (1966–1967).

Fontenrose, Joseph. *The Ritual Theory of Myth*. Berkeley, 1966.

Forman, Werner, and Bjamba Rintschen. *Lamaistische Tanzmasken: Der Erlik-Tsam in der Mongolei*. Leipzig, n.d.

Fox, J. Robin. "Witchcraft and Clanship in Cochiti Therapy," *Magic, Witchcraft, and Curing*. Ed. John Middleton. Garden City, 1967.

Frazer, Sir James George. *The New Golden Bough*. Ed. Theodor H. Gaster. New York, 1959.

Frothingham, A. L. "The Babylonian Origin of Hermes the Snake-God, and of the Caduceus," *American Journal of Archeology*, 20 (1916).

Gargi, Balwant. *Folk Theater of India*. Seattle and London, 1966.

Gaster, Theodor H. *Thespis: Ritual, Myth, and Drama in the Ancient Near East*. Garden City, 1950.

Gelfand, Michael. *Shona Ritual: With Special Reference to the Chaminuka Cult*. Capetown, 1959.

Ghosh, Manomohan, trans. *The Nātyaśāstra, A Treatise on Hindu Dramaturgy and Histrionics, Ascribed to Bharata-muni*. 2 vols. Calcutta, 1961.

Goldman, Hetty. "The Origin of the Greek Herm," *American Journal*

Laufer, Berthold. *Oriental Theatricals*. Chicago, 1923.

Lawler, Lillian B. *The Dance in Ancient Greece*. Middletown, Connecticut, 1964.

Lee, Peter H. *Korean Literature: Topics and Themes*. Tucson, 1965.

Lee, Richard B. (S) "The Sociology of !Kung Bushman Trance Performances," *Trance and Possession States*. Ed. Raymond Prince. Montreal, 1966.

———. (T) "Trance Cure of the !Kung Bushmen," *Natural History*, 76:9 (November 1967).

Lévi-Strauss, Claude. *Totemism*. Trans. Rodney Needham. Boston, 1963.

Lewis, I. M. *Ecstatic Religion: An Anthropological Study of Spirit Possession and Shamanism*. Middlesex, England, 1971.

Lindsay, Jack. *The Clashing Rocks*. London, 1965.

Lombard, Frank Alanson. *An Outline History of the Japanese Drama*. c. 1928; rpt. New York, 1966.

Lommel, Andreas. (M) *Masks: Their Meaning and Function*. New York, 1970.

———. (S) *Shamanism: The Beginnings of Art*. Trans. Michael Bullock. New York, 1967.

———. *The World of the Early Hunters*. London, 1967. (Identical with *Shamanism*.)

Mace, Carroll Edward. *Two Spanish-Quiché Dance Dramas of Rabinal*. New Orleans, 1971.

Mackerras, Colin. (G) "The Growth of the Chinese Regional Drama in the Ming and Ch'ing," *Journal of Oriental Studies*, 9:1 (January 1971).

———. *The Rise of the Peking Opera: 1770–1870. Social Aspects of the Theatre in Manchu China*. Oxford, 1972.

Marshall, Lorna. "The Medicine Dance of the !King Bushmen," *Africa* (London) 39:4 (October 1969).

Menagh, H. B. "The Question of Primitive Origins," *Educational Theatre Journal*, 15:3 (October. 1963).

Messenger, John C. "Ibibio Drama," *Africa*, 41:3 (1971).

Métraux, Alfred. *Voodoo in Haiti*. Trans. Hugh Charteris. New York, 1972 (1959).

Muller, Werner. "North America," Walter Krickeberg, Hermann Trimborn, Werner Muller, Otto Zerries. *Pre-Columbian American Religions*. Trans. Stanley Davis. New York, 1968.

Murray, Gilbert. "Excursus on the Ritual Forms Preserved in Greek

Tragedy," Jane Ellen Harrison. *Themis: A Study of the Social Origins of Greek Religion.* New York, 1927.

——. (R) "Ritual Elements in the New Comedy," *Classical Quarterly*, 27 (January–April 1943).

Nilsson, Martin P. *The Minoan-Mycenaean Religion and its Survival in Greek Religion.* Oxford, 1927.

Obeyesekere, Gananath. "The Ritual Drama of the *Sanni* Demons: Collective Representations of Disease in Ceylon," *Comparative Studies in Society and History*, 11:2 (April 1969).

O'Neill, P. G. *Early Nō Drama: Its Background, Character and Development 1300–1450.* London, 1958.

Onghokham. "The Wayang Topèng World of Malang," *Indonesia*, 14 (October 1972).

Otto, Walter. *Dionysus: Myth and Cult.* Trans. Robert B. Palmer. Bloomington, Indiana, 1965.

Parker, H. *Ancient Ceylon: An Account of the Aborigines and of Part of the Early Civilization.* London, 1909.

Parsons, Elsie Clews, and Ralph L. Beals. "The Sacred Clowns of the Pueblo and Mayo-Yaqui Indians," *American Anthropologist*, 36:4 (October–December 1934).

Pascal, R. "On the Origins of the Liturgical Drama of the Middle Ages," *Modern Language Review*, 36:3 (July 1941).

Pattanaik, Dhirendra Nath. "A Note on Hastas," *Classical and Folk Dances of India.* Bombay, 1963.

Pe-Chin, Chang. *Chinese Opera and Painted Face.* Taipei, 1969.

Perkins, P. D. and Keiichi Fujii. "Kagura, A Ceremonial Dance of Japan," *Cultural Nippon*, 7 (April 1939).

Pertold, O. "The Ceremonial Dances of the Sinhalese: An Inquiry into the Sinhalese Folk-Religion," *Archiv Orientálnī*, Vol. 2, 1930.

Philippi, Donald L., trans. *Kojiki.* Princeton and Tokyo, 1969.

Pickard-Cambridge, Sir Arthur. *Dithyramb, Tragedy and Comedy.* 2d ed. revised by T. B. L. Webster. Oxford, 1962.

——. (F) *The Dramatic Festivals of Athens.* Oxford, 1953.

Pisharoti, K. R. "South Indian Theatre," H. H. Wilson, V. Ragavan, K. R. Pisharoti, Amulya Charan Vidybhusan, *The Theatre of the Hindus.* Delhi, n.d.

Plato. *Laws.* Trans. R. G. Bury. Cambridge, Massachusetts, 1961.

Plutarch. *Moralia.* Trans. Frank Cole Babbitt. 15 vols. Cambridge, Massachusetts, 1962.

Popov, A. "Consecration Ritual for a Blacksmith Novice among the

Wavell, Stewart. "Through the Fire of Existence to the Needles of Eternity," Stewart Wavell, Audrey Butt, Nina Epton, *Trances*. London, 1966.

Weil, Peter M. "The Masked Figure and Social Control: The Mandinka Case," *Africa*, 41:4 (1971).

Wilson, Edward Meryan. "An Unpublished Version of the Pace-Eggers' Play," *Folk-Lore*, 49 (March 1938).

Wirz, Paul. *Exorcism and the Art of Healing in Ceylon*. Leiden, 1954.

Wood, Melusine. "Sticks, Handkerchiefs and Horses in India," *Journal of the English Folk Dance and Song Society*, 5 (December 1946).

Wu-chi, Liu. *An Introduction to Chinese Literature*. Bloomington, 1966.

Yalman, Nur. "The Structure of Sinhalese Healing Rituals," *Religion in South Asia*. Ed. Edward B. Harper. Seattle, 1964.

Yen, Joseph C. Y. "A Study in Detail of the Acting Roles of the Peking Theatre," *Chinese Culture*, 12:2 (1971).

Ze-ami. *Kadensho*. Sakurai Chuichi et al., trans. Kyoto, 1968.

Zerries, Otto. "Primitive South America and the West Indies," Walter Krickeberg, Hermann Trimborn, Werner Müller, Otto Zerries, *Pre-Columbian American American Religions*. Trans. Stanley Davis. New York, 1968.

Zucker, A. E. *The Chinese Theatre*. Boston, 1925.

Zung, Cecilia S. L. *Secrets of the Chinese Drama*. New York, 1964 (1937).